MW00425398

A KID FROM MARLBORO ROAD

a novel

EDWARD BURNS

SEVEN STORIES PRESS
NEW YORK / OAKLAND / LONDON

*To my mother and father, and to their parents and
grandparents, who crossed the Atlantic with nothing in
their pockets but hopes and dreams.*

∽

Copyright © 2024 Edward Burns

Seven Stories Press
140 Watts Street
New York, NY 10013
www.sevenstories.com

Library of Congress Cataloging-in-Publication Data

Names: Burns, Edward, 1968- author.
Title: A kid from Marlboro Road : a novel / Edward Burns.
Description: New York : Seven Stories Press, 2024.
Identifiers: LCCN 2024006923 | ISBN 9781644214077 (hardcover) | ISBN
   9781644214084 (ebook)
Subjects: LCGFT: Novels.
Classification: LCC PS3552.U732438 K54 2024
LC record available at https://lccn.loc.gov/2024006923

College professors and high school and middle school teachers may order free examination
copies of Seven Stories Press titles. Visit https://www.sevenstories.com/pg/resources-
academics or email academic@sevenstories.com.

Printed in the United States of America

9 8 7 6 5 4 3 2 1

Contents

A KID FROM MARLBORO ROAD

1

We went to Pop's wake today. It was an open coffin service which means exactly what it sounds like. I'd never seen a dead person before and my grandfather would be the first. You wait on line to take your turn going up to the casket so you can kneel and say a prayer. My mom was already there, standing next to the coffin and flowers, with her brothers Mike and Mark and her stepmother Gilligan. I couldn't even look at her because she was so upset. I'd already been crying for two days now and didn't want to start again in front of all these strangers.

The place was packed. There were forty rows of chairs and every seat was filled. There was a line of people waiting to pay their respects that went all the way out the front door and onto the sidewalk. It wasn't only our family and Pop's friends from the Bronx. There were hundreds of the sandhogs, guys who must have come straight from work because they were still wearing muddy work boots and dirty work pants and had greasy work gloves stuffed into their back pockets and hard hats in their hands. There were cops in uniform and detectives in nice suits. There were old Irish biddies dressed in black who sat quietly praying with their rosary beads and other old Irish biddies who cried out loud. There were the men from the bar where Pop used to drink every night and the sole surviving friend from his kitchen who used to sing and dance with Pop on Saturday nights.

"You see this crowd, that's the sign of a well-liked man," my dad said.

"So it is," I replied, trying to do Pop's Irish accent.

My father smiled, took my hand and held it. It felt good even if his hand was sweaty. I'm not embarrassed to hold his hand in public today because it's a funeral and I'm sad and no one makes fun of a kid at his grandfather's funeral. He kept holding it until someone started talking to him and pulled him away, leaving me and Tommy alone on the line. Tommy seems like a different kid since we got the news that Pop died. He's not a dick anymore. He's nice to my parents, asks if he can help out around the house, and even said he could look after me when we're at the wake. But the weird thing is I haven't seen him cry at all. I was watching him when we got close to the coffin and he didn't even look that sad.

"Do you know what to do?" I asked him.

"Yeah, you just go up there and kneel down and say a prayer."

"Do you want to go up there together?" I asked.

"Yeah, maybe we should," he said.

So that's what we did. After we knelt down, we did the sign of the cross and bowed our heads. I was having a tough time thinking of a prayer to say because I was too busy looking at Pop's face. I mean, it looked like my grandpa, and it didn't. It's hard to describe. It's almost like he looked fake and not dead but maybe that's what a dead person looks like. He was also wearing a suit and tie and I had never seen him dressed up before.

When Tommy finished his prayer, he reached out and touched Pop's hand and said, "Let's go." I couldn't believe he touched him. Now I wanted to touch him too, but Tommy had already stood up and said, "Come on, people are waiting." So I had to get up. I hate to admit this, but I was jealous he got to touch a dead person and I didn't. I'm sure it's a sin to think that.

After we got up, we went to the receiving line and first said hello to Uncle Mike, who was standing next to the coffin. Uncle Mike is big and strong and wasn't crying. He shook our hands and gave us a hug and told us Pop is in a better place. Uncle Mark was next to him and he looked like he'd been crying but he made a joke about how funny we look in our cheap suits. He didn't shake our hands or give us a hug but instead pretended to punch Tommy in the stomach and messed up my hair. My mom was next on the receiving line. The minute I saw her, I grabbed her around the waist, squeezing her as hard as I could, and started crying. I don't know why that happened but I couldn't control it. She tried to tell me everything's OK, but she couldn't because she was crying too and was probably having trouble speaking because I was squeezing her so hard. That's when Tommy decided to be a dick and just walked out of the funeral home, not even saying anything to our mom or Gilligan. I wanted to kill him.

After mom wiped the tears from my face and I gave Gilligan a hug, I walked through the crowd looking for Tommy and I was getting so mad that I said to myself, *When I find him, I'm not gonna say anything to him, I'm just gonna walk up to him and punch him in his mean face.* Then I saw him. He was sitting in a chair in the middle of the back row of the funeral home. He was stuck between two old biddies in black who were saying their rosaries and he was crying, like really crying with a red face and his whole body heaving up and down.

After the wake, we all walked across the street to a bar and everyone was in a much better mood. Even my mom was smiling and laughing as she told everyone about Pop taking her to the bars on Third Avenue while he had his pints and sang his songs, so he did, and she would sit on the bar and wait for him to finish his antics and throw her onto his shoulders so they could head uptown to the next bar. Everyone laughed and toasted and shouted Pop's name and they drank their drinks and told more stories.

The one sole surviving Irish musician from Pop's kitchen sing-alongs, Brady, the fiddle player, raised his glass and said, "Let this be for the soul of Pop McSweeny."

Everyone raised their glass.

"May it be received," they responded before they drank.

Gilligan told everyone that she thought Pop must have known the Lord would be calling for him soon.

"Wouldn't you know, when I went to look for his suit to be buried in, I couldn't find it anywhere until I closed the bedroom door and there it was on the hook and it had just come from the dry cleaner's a few days earlier," Gilligan said. "Mind you, this is a suit he hadn't worn in twenty years, and why would a man get the urge to send a suit that he hadn't worn in twenty years to the dry cleaner's unless the Lord had given him a sign and touched his shoulder and whispered in his ear that the suit was in need of a press? Because if you're going to be meeting our savior you can't be wearing a wrinkled suit."

There was silence after she told that story and all of Pop's friends and family nodded. My Uncle Mark then turned to me and asked if I'd like to say a few words or tell a story. I shook my head.

"Come on, kid. If you can't tell a halfway entertaining story about one of the funniest men you'll ever meet then you've got no right to stand at this bar or be part of this family." I looked to my dad and he shrugged.

"Your Uncle Mark is right. Tell us one thing you remember about your grandfather."

I couldn't believe my dad was doing this to me. I didn't know most of these people and wasn't even supposed to be allowed in the bar, but I had no choice.

"OK," I said. "There was this one story Pop told me that he thought was so funny, he told it to me a bunch of times. He said the night my dad proposed to my mom, he and my mom went out to celebrate and they were sitting in a booth at a bar and my mom was crying."

Uncle Mike jumped in, "She's always been given to the tears, hasn't she?" The people that knew her well all nodded.

I said, "But this time she was crying because she was happy. But then somebody told you guys, her brothers, that they saw your sister in the bar down the street crying. So, you two ran in there and didn't ask any questions—you grabbed my dad and dragged him outside and were about to beat him up when my mom ran out screaming at you to stop, and she had to show you the ring to prove that she was crying happy tears and not sad tears. And then all four of you walked up the block to the apartment to wake up Pop and tell him the good news but he was out drinking. So, you had to go to every bar in the Bronx to find him and when you finally did, he looked at the engagement ring my dad gave my mom and he just shook his head and said, 'That won't do, so it won't.' And you all walked back up the Concourse to the apartment and Pop took out Grandma's old engagement ring and gave that to my dad, even though it wasn't as nice as the ring my dad got my mom because Pop got Grandma that ring when they still lived in Ireland and were really poor. And then my dad had to re-propose in front of all of you in the kitchen and that's it. That's all I remember."

I didn't get any laughs because it's not really a funny story, but I was told I was allowed to stick around. My mom then had to show everybody the ring and as she did the smile from their wedding album returned to her face.

2

So, I was sitting on my bed one night looking at the big maple tree outside my window. It was a windy night and most of the leaves had fallen off and these thick nasty-looking branches were reaching out in all directions, going this way and that way, whipping back and forth, and there was this one branch that was scratching the outside wall of my room.

When I was a real little kid, that scratching sound would scare the shit out of me. And if I'm being honest with you, it can still be pretty scary now but I'm too old to run into my parents' room and get into bed with them.

Except sometimes, when my dad is working midnights, I still sneak in to sleep with my mom. We listen to this radio show she loves, Jean Shepherd. He's this guy that sings silly songs and tells stories and it's really good for falling asleep to. I love the stories about when he was a kid. If he's telling a really good one, like the one about being a paper boy, me and my mom will stay up till 11:30 p.m. when he goes off the air just so we can hear how it ends. If she's getting tired and turns off the radio before one of his stories is over, she'll ask me if I'm still awake and I'll pretend to be sleeping so I don't have to go back to my bed. I used to be able to sleep in her bed all the time but now that I'm older she says I need to learn how to sleep on my own. I tell her I already know how to sleep on my own, but I'd rather sleep in her bed and listen to Jean Shepherd.

"But you have your own radio in your own room. Listen to Jean Shepherd in there," she tells me, but she doesn't understand it's more fun to listen with her so that we can laugh together and talk about the parts of the story we liked best.

Those are probably my favorite times with my mom, and I know they're her favorite times with me because every time we do it, she hugs and kisses me like I'm still a little kid and calls me Kneeney and tells me these are her favorite times with me. The Jean Shepherd show always starts with this song that sounds like the racetrack when the horses are going to the gate. The call to the post. If I hear that bugle call coming from her room and my dad's not home, that's my signal to sneak in. I'm like one of the horses at Belmont—time to leave the paddock.

I know a little bit about horse racing because we live close to the Belmont Park racetrack where they hold the Belmont Stakes, and because my dad loves to "play the ponies." Every year in the fall, me and my brother Tommy will go with him and some of the cops he works with to the fall meets. There's a big event at the meets called the Marlboro. My dad says it's our lucky race since we live on Marlboro Road. And he's right. Every time we go to the track for the Marlboro Meet, we win.

I love our days at the track and not just because betting on races is fun but because my dad's partner on the cops, Carmine Cappabianco, knows one of the trainers and we always get to go down to the stables with him and see the horses up close. Once, I even got to sit on one of them. We bet on Carmine's friend's horse that day, but he lost. Tommy said that's why we were allowed to sit on him. "He had no shot of winning. They'd never let you sit on a winner."

So, like I was saying, I was sitting in bed, looking out the window because usually there's something interesting happening on the street corner. We live at the intersection of Marlboro Road and Page Road and the corner across the street from our house is a major hangout for the older teenagers in our neighborhood. Depending on the time of day or the season of the year, there's always something fun to watch. There's this one couple, Linda Leary and Paulie Fontana, who always show up around eleven o'clock when most of the others have taken off and these two will sit on the curb under the streetlight and make out for hours. And I mean literally, for hours! I know this because I've watched them a bunch of times. There have been nights when I've gone to the bathroom or went to talk to my mom to see what show she's watching or one time I even fell asleep for a few hours and when I looked out the window again, there they were, Linda and Paulie, still going at it. I haven't kissed anybody yet, but I can't imagine wanting to do it for hours at a time.

But that night, it's windy and cold out and the corner is quiet and I'm getting sleepy when I suddenly remembered I had to hand in this English assignment the next day. Like with most of my homework, I'd waited to do it until the night before it was due. You see, I'm not great at being a student. I mean, I'm not a moron and I get OK grades and I'm not one of those kids that just hates going to class. When it comes to school, I could take it or leave it. But when you're in sixth grade, you have to take it, right?

Anyhow, my homework was I had to write a poem and what made it really suck even worse than a normal poetry assignment was it had to be about Jesus. I go to a Catholic school, by the way: St. Joes. So, this wasn't the first time I had to figure out words that rhyme with Jesus. Breezes is one of my go-tos. And wheezes. And sneezes. And cheeses. You get the idea. It's hard. But poems with sneezes and cheeses and wheezes don't go over too well with the nuns. If you went to a school that had nuns, then you'd know what I'm talking about. That's where the big maple comes in.

I'm watching the tree's branches sway back and forth in the wind and all the smaller branches are reaching out toward the sky like little tentacles and I get this idea that this old tree is Jesus. I imagine that the maple tree struggling in the storm is like Jesus struggling to speak to people in a screwed-up world. The branches reaching out into the terrible windy night are like Jesus's hands reaching out into the terrible sad world to heal people and make them feel better when they're scared or lonely or, if they're like my mom, sad that the world is changing. The big thick trunk of the tree shows how strong Jesus is and kinda represents his heart and soul. And all the roots are his words and prayers reaching down into the earth for people to find when they're farming their fields or making sandcastles on the beach or digging for worms to go fishing or making holes in the street for new sewers or building a basement for a building, you know, basically anything that people do with the dirt of the earth. Anyhow, that was kinda the idea.

I know it sounds stupid but in the poem it sounded better because it all rhymed, except this time I didn't rhyme anything with Jesus. And it was a poem, so it didn't really need to make sense, right? It just needed to sound good and give you a feeling, which I think it did.

So, I hand in this lame assignment the next day and didn't think about it again. I figure I'll get a B minus if I'm lucky but I might get a C because I didn't proofread it and I'm a terrible speller and I have really shitty handwriting. Talk about something the nuns hate. Bad handwriting. You would think it's one of the seven deadly sins the way they go crazy over it.

When my mom and dad went to Catholic school they said the nuns were even tougher than the nuns we got at St. Joes, which is hard to imagine, until they tell you the stories about getting cracked on the knuckles with the ruler if you had shitty handwriting. Or worse than that, they'd crack the boys behind their legs with that skinny wooden stick they use when they're showing you the different countries on the map or pointing to the different presidents' pictures that hang above the blackboard. My dad said he got it so bad one time that the backs of his thighs were bleeding, and he had to spend all day at school sitting at his desk while the blood dried. When he finally got up at the end of the day, his school pants were stuck to the scabs on his legs. He knew he couldn't tell his mother because the old Irish back then didn't believe the nuns or the priests could ever do any wrong, even if they made you bleed.

"If I told my mother, she woulda said I musta deserved it and given me an even worse beating for upsetting the nuns in the first place," my dad said.

He had a real problem on his hands when he got home from school that day because when he tried to take his pants off he couldn't do it without ripping those scabs off, which he said would have hurt worse than the beating. So, his brother, my Uncle Tim, suggested they fill the tub with water and my dad could sit in there to soften up the scabs. But they realized if he did that, their mother was sure to see the blood in the tub and on the towels and find out about the beating so they decided they would walk over to the river and jump in. The problem was it was January in New York and to jump off the pier on the West Side of Manhattan wasn't like jumping into the Mississippi River like Tom Sawyer and Huck Finn.

"You were likely to land on some poor slob that some wiseguy decided to dump in the river—or you'd freeze to death," my dad said.

So instead, my Uncle Tim volunteered to piss on his legs and that's when my dad knew he had to go home and tell his mother the truth because getting pissed on or jumping onto a dead wiseguy in the freezing cold Hudson River had to be worse than catching a beating.

They lived in Hell's Kitchen, where my grandmother still lives, and as they walked home they passed a stable on Tenth Avenue where they noticed the horses drinking out of a trough and they both knew that was the solution. As my Uncle Tim kept lookout, my dad jumped into that trough and sat there until he could peel his pants off. Then the two of them ran down to Forty-Eighth Street, my father in just his underwear and my uncle behind him, laughing the whole way home. But then, as they ran up the stoop and into the apartment, who did they run into? Their mother. My dad laughs about it now but he said, "For a tiny little lady, she could pack a wallop. And that was the worst beating she ever gave me."

3

There's this one old guy on our block, Mr. Ford, and he has a 1957 Chevy Corvette. And it's a goddamn convertible!

Mr. Ford is a funny old geezer who sometimes invites me and my friends into his garage when he's working on the Vette. And every time he does, my friend Gerry always asks him the same question.

"How come you bought a Chevy if your last name is Ford?"

I mean, every single time we go over there, Gerry asks that same stupid question. And he's not trying to be funny or a wise guy, he's just not that smart.

"Son, if the Ford Motor Company made the Corvette, I'd own a Ford," Mr. Ford always answers.

I don't know why he even bothers answering Gerry. I'd tell him to stop asking me the same goddamn stupid question every time I see him, but I guess Mr. Ford is nicer than me.

Old Man Ford is a real Mr. Fix It and loves to show us the engine of the Vette, which he's painted red and white to match the red-and-white leather seats and red-and-white dash and dials. He tells us you want to keep your car's engine so clean you could eat your lunch off of it. He likes to give little lessons like that.

He'll tell us, "It's important to have the right tools, but more important to use them the right way."

When he starts with the advice and cornball stuff like that is when we tell him we have to be home for dinner. But that's what old timers do, right? They give you corny advice whether you asked for it or not.

Last week when we were hanging around his driveway, he had just finished a new project he was working on. He took an old lawn mower engine and somehow fixed it onto this weird old bicycle he has. This bike had to be from World War II or maybe even the Great Depression, because you've never seen a big old bike like this before, other than in an old movie like *Butch Cassidy and the Sundance Kid* maybe. You know that scene where the one guy has the girl on the handlebars and they get chased by the bull and they're playing the "Raindrops Keep Falling on My Head" song? It's a bike like that.

Anyway, now that Old Man Ford has this engine on this crazy bike, he doesn't have to peddle anymore. He just pulls the chord on that lawn mower engine and off he goes, which is good because he rides that bike all over, sometimes going all the way to Rockaway Beach which is a pretty far ride from our neighborhood. I only know that because my great-grandmother, Svenska, has a summer bungalow in Rockaway and when I go to visit her, I sometimes see Mr. Ford cruising around the boardwalk. Me and my friends have ridden our bikes to Rockaway and it's a haul so I can imagine if you're as old as Mr. Ford, you'd probably have a friggin' heart attack trying to get there if you didn't have an engine on your bike. I should tell you that Mr. Ford has got to be almost eighty or ninety years old. And skinny. With that old man skin that you can see through. It's as thin as the wax paper they use to wrap up your sandwich at the deli, so you can see all his veins, which is real nasty to look at when he takes his shirt off in the summer. I don't know why old guys do that. There should be a law that says after you turn forty or something, you have to keep your shirt on in public.

My mom jokes that Mr. Ford must have a girlfriend he meets under the boardwalk out there because why else would he go through all the effort. But I think there's no way an old guy like him has a girlfriend. And if he does, that's just too gross to even think about, especially when you imagine him taking his shirt off, which you have to do when you have a girlfriend.

Sometimes after dinner my dad walks across the street to have a beer with Mr. Ford. He likes to hear the old stories about the neighborhood and what our town used to be like. My dad loves old stories.

He says, "I'm just a reminiscing fool. It's the Irish in me."

Mr. Ford told my dad that he was the first person to live in his house and moved in the day the last carpenter left.

"Me and my family came here from the city to get some fresh air for the kids and a garage for me to do some tinkering in," Mr. Ford told my dad. My dad told Mr. Ford that's the same reason we left Queens, but my dad isn't really a tinkerer. A tinkerer tinkers for fun, my dad just fixes stuff that gets broken, which is usually one of our old shitty cars.

It's sad, but by the time we moved into our house, Mr. Ford's wife had died and whatever kids he had stopped coming to visit him, which is probably why he always invites us neighborhood kids over to watch him work. That would really suck if you were a nice old guy like him and your kids never came to visit you. And it makes no sense because Mr. Ford seems like he was probably a good dad. He's nice and he never curses and never drinks, which is why it can make you sad to think of him spending all those days and nights alone in that house. Hopefully, my mom is right, and he does have a girlfriend in Rockaway.

Mr. Ford says that our town used to be a big old farm until the county laid down the Long Island Rail Road tracks right through the middle of it so that people from the city could get out to Rockaway Beach in the summertime. Then, this farmer that owned the land got pissed and sold the whole place to this guy named Gibson, who wanted to turn the farm into a little village. So this Gibson guy convinced whoever it is who makes these kinds of decisions to build a train station here as well. And they did. That's why they named the town and the train station after this Gibson guy, which makes sense since this whole neighborhood was his idea, right? So that's the story of our town, Gibson.

If you've ever been on the Long Island Rail Road and you were bored and looking out the window at all the houses zipping by, then you've probably seen towns like Gibson where all the houses kinda look the same. Blocks and blocks of these skinny little houses with tight little driveways between them, and tiny little backyards behind them, with their tidy little lawns out front, and each with its own maple tree planted on that strip of grass between the sidewalk and the gutter.

What Mr. Gibson didn't realize when he planted these maples in front of every house was that, when maple trees grow, their roots don't grow down into the dirt, they grow up and bubble out and over the ground, pushing up the sidewalks and curbs and streets, breaking through the concrete and making cracks in all different directions. I know my dad worries when I leave my bike blocking the path on the sidewalk for the old biddies walking home from the Lutheran church, but those cracks in the sidewalk are much more dangerous, if you're asking me.

When we were little, we used to play that game "Step on a crack, break your momma's back," where'd you'd try to walk down the street without touching a crack on the sidewalk, but it was impossible on our street because of all the damage the maple trees and their roots did. There was this one spot in front of the Dabrowski's house, which is halfway down the block between my house and my best friend Louie's, where the roots had pushed the sidewalk up to create a giant ten-inch ramp. Me and Louie loved that broken sidewalk in front of the Dabrowski's house because we used it as a jump for our bikes, but everybody else thought it was an accident waiting to happen, especially the old biddies. The neighbors tried to convince Mrs. Dabrowski to have her husband cut the tree down, dig out the roots and fix the sidewalk but she said it was the town's job, not her husband's.

The Dabrowski maple finally came down after Mrs. Van Warren tripped on the big chunk of sidewalk outside the Dabrowski's house and fell. She didn't break her back, but she did crack her head open. Mrs. Van Warren is one of the old biddies that lives on our street. There's a few of these old ladies left on my block and my dad says they've been here forever, from when they first built these houses in the 1920s. The early settlers, he calls them.

After the ambulance took Mrs. Van Warren away, her next-door neighbor, Mr. O'Neil, took his chainsaw to the Dabrowski maple and we all watched as it fell into the middle of the street blocking traffic for a few hours until Mr. O'Neil cut it up into logs and had his boys haul off all that wood to their house.

The O'Neils live down the block from me. They're one of these really big Irish families with ten kids. We've got a lot of families like that around here. And it's not just the Irish families but the Italians too. We got the Dillons with twelve, the Rubinos with ten, the DeLeas with thirteen, and the Murphys with fourteen. And those are just the double-digits families. There are plenty others who have seven, eight, and nine kids. I think it would be awesome to have that many brothers and sisters because if you're like me and you only have one brother and he's a jerk, you're shit out of luck, but if you have eight boys in your family like the Murphys, then odds are at least one of your brothers will be nice to you.

The houses in Gibson are all the same. They have one bigger bedroom for your parents and two small bedrooms for the kids. But because everyone has these huge families, most people turn their attics and basements into bedrooms too—though in the summer the attics get as hot as an oven and when you've got six of your eight boys living up there together, like the Murphys do, you can imagine how sticky and smelly that room must get. So, in the summer, the Murphy's set up tents all over their property. They got tents pitched in their side yard, their front yard and even in the driveway and that's where the Murphy boys sleep. When you ride by on your bike on a summer day, it looks like a campground. You can see them all hanging out in their tents, and it seems like so much fun but whenever I ask my dad if we can set up a tent in our backyard, he tells me to go ask your mother.

When I ask her, she tells me, "You can sleep in a tent when

you go camping, but I will not have this house looking like that shanty town up the street."

With all these families with all these kids, you can imagine what a summer night is like on our block and every other block in the neighborhood. It's nothing but kids everywhere you turn and most of the time that's great because you can always find someone to play with. Sometimes, though, it's not so great because if you turned onto the wrong block on the wrong night, there's a good chance you'll get your ass kicked, so you got to know what blocks are safe and what blocks to stay away from. Lucky for us, our block is pretty safe because of the O'Neil boys. They're not like most tough guys because they're actually nice and instead of kicking your ass when they see you, they say, "What's up little man," and if you're getting picked on, they'll step in and scare the shit out of the bullies. They're almost like having your own police force on the block.

"They look like a pack of farmers," is what my dad says about them because they all have red hair and huge thick arms and wide shoulders and lots of freckles. They're also great at every sport they play. Andy was a football star, Joe was a basketball star, Larry and Doug were the wrestlers, and Kevin and Billy were the baseball heroes. But Big Ray, the boxer, was the oldest and Ray was a legend. He was so much of a legend that that's what he's called—The Legend. He has to be close to twenty-five now and nobody ever messes with The Legend.

The Legend was famous for beating up a grown man when he was just sixteen and that's how he got his nickname. Some jerk was hassling a lady who used to live on the block. She was divorced and rented out a basement apartment in the Di

Vincenzo's house. One night, The Legend was walking home from the park and saw the divorced lady get pushed to the sidewalk by this jerky guy. My mom said she was probably on one of her many dates. Anyway, The Legend sees this and asks the lady if she's OK and the guy says, "Get the fuck outta here, kid, unless you want to get your face rearranged." The Legend didn't say anything back to the guy, he just walked over and punched the guy in the face. With one shot, the guy was laid out, stone cold. You do something like that and you become a legend.

The Legend led the rest of the freckled, red-headed, all-star O'Neil boys as they threw those massive pieces of tree trunk on their shoulders, carried them down the street, up their driveway and into their backyard. It was like an invasion of the lumberjacks onto our Long Island street. For years, the O'Neils chopped that wood for their fireplace and every winter when you walked past their house you could smell it burning. And is there anything better than the smell of burning wood on a winter night? After that, anytime we smelled the O'Neil's fireplace we would say, "The Dabrowski maple burns again."

Most of the old maples that lined our block are gone now and before you know it there will be none of them left and that makes my mom sad. It seems to me, my mom is sad a lot of the time these days, and this was even before Pop died. She always used to be laughing and joking and dancing, but these days she drifts off into a quiet place. And it can be things like the fact that so many of the maple trees have died that set her off.

"It just breaks your heart, doesn't it," she'll say. And you can see in her eyes that it really is breaking her heart and when you're a kid and you see that look in your mom's eyes it's scary and confusing. So you look away.

One day this fall as we turned onto our block she started in. "When we first bought the house, you should have seen what the neighborhood looked like. You'd drive down the street and every block was lined with big beautiful trees with all their leaves changing colors. Red, yellow, and orange. It looked like the sky was on fire."

My dad says, "If Mr. Gibson would have planted sycamores, like they did on Corchoran Boulevard, your heart wouldn't be breaking today."

I guess sycamores can live to be about five hundred years old or something and their roots grow straight down into the ground and don't mess up your sidewalks causing old biddies like Mrs. Van Warren to trip and fall and be raced off to the hospital with a cracked skull. But not the maples.

"Planted in the twenties, dying in the seventies, like so many other things," my mom says. She then made comparisons to a lot of stuff she thought used to be great and beautiful but have fallen apart in the 1970s.

"The subways, Times Square, the Grand Concourse, even Rockaway Beach." Then with a tear rolling down her cheek, she says, "The world of my childhood is disappearing before my eyes."

She mentions all those places because my mom grew up in the Bronx and used to take the subway from her apartment off the Concourse to Rockaway Beach, which is where she met my dad before they had their first proper date at a theater in Times Square to see Frank Sinatra. She says none of those places look the same as they used to, and she gets the sad look in her eyes when she says it. My dad then teases her by singing that song about Joe D. That's how he tries to cheer you up—by teasing you.

"If I take the piss out of you, maybe you'll stop feeling so sorry for yourself," he says. It works sometimes. Other times, it can make you feel worse. Today, it seems to work on my mom.

"Where have you gone, Joe DiMaggio? Our nation turns its lonely eyes to you. What's that you say, Mrs. Robinson? Jolting Joe has left and gone away."

They both love that song because they both love Joe DiMaggio and they love the Yankees and the guys who sing that song are from Queens and who doesn't love hometown heroes.

This cheers my mom up and she smiles at him and tells him to stop making fun of her and they both laugh. I sit in the back seat of the car listening to every word because it's good to see them laughing together again. I can't remember when they stopped laughing together but it doesn't happen too much anymore. Maybe that's why my mom seems so sad all the time. Or maybe it's because—just like she says—the world is changing before her eyes. And it's not just all the places from when she was young, it's also Tommy and me.

"I miss my little momma's boys," she'll say. "Those cute little guys who loved nothing better than sitting on their mother's knee. What happened to those guys?" she sometimes asks me. I want to tell her that, like Jolting Joe, those momma's boys have up and gone away. But I never say it because that would make her feel even worse.

After we park outside the house, we get out of the car and look up at our old maple and my dad says, "Well, you don't have to worry about our tree, that thing won't come down for a long time."

4

A few days later, I get the Jesus poem back and I get an A plus. I'm in shock because I don't get a lot of A pluses. But then my teacher tells me I'm going to need to see the Bull after class. That's what we call our principal, Sister Peter Margret. Now I'm terrified because I'm thinking maybe it's a sin to compare Jesus to a tree. Who knows? So, I'm sitting in the Bull's office and of course I'm watching her closely because I'm expecting a smack, because why else do you get called to the principal's office, but instead she smiles. The Bull actually smiles. I don't think I've ever seen her teeth before or since and like the rest of her, they look mean, all yellow and crooked. But then here's the real shocker. After she smiles, she tells me she's proud of me. She had no idea I was so thoughtful and in concert with Jesus and his message—whatever the heck that means. Then she kills me with this next one.

"I'd like to submit your poem to the Catholic Daughters of America Poetry Contest this year, if that's alright with you?"

If that's alright with you? "Hell no, that is not alright with me," is what I want to say but you can't say that to a nun, especially the Bull, so I just shrug and say something stupid like, "Yeah, sure, OK, I guess so."

Now this is where the story gets crazy. The Bull sends in the poem, and the poem wins the contest and then me and my parents have to go to an awards ceremony at the Knights of Columbus. Then to make things worse than they already were, they give me a trophy for it. A trophy for a poem? Who ever heard of such a thing? And it's twice as big as any of my trophies from baseball and basketball and when I put it on my trophy shelf it makes all my other trophies look so small and lame that I hide it in my closet until my mother finds it and brings this giant thing down to the living room and puts it on the bookcase so everybody and their mother can see it. When Grandma from the City, that's what we call my dad's mom, the one I just told you about who packs the wallop, comes over to stay with us one weekend, which she does every couple of months, she sees the trophy and is so proud she won't shut up about how it's a sure sign I must be a candidate for the priesthood.

"Over my dead body," my dad says. "This kid is gonna be some kinda writer."

Just so you know, I'm not going to share the poem with you, even if it isn't half bad. Not that you had your heart set on it or anything, but I'm not going through that abuse again. You got to understand, writing poems and reading poetry are surefire ways to get your ass kicked and it's bad enough when they publish this thing in the church bulletin and kids from school start reading it because when you're bored outta your mind during Mass you'll read anything to make the time pass, which means almost everybody read this stupid thing, because the only thing to read in church is the church bulletin. You can't imagine the shit I got after that. That first Monday at school, some kids, mostly eighth graders, decide I must be some kinda brownnose for winning a poetry contest which means I deserved a smack to the head and a punch in the shoulder with a purple nurple to top it off—that's when they grab one of your nipples and twist it. And if a teacher sees you getting smacked or punched or nurpled, they just assume you were fighting and send you down to the Bull's office and like I already told you, if you got sent to the Bull you better be ready for one of her smacks even if you did just win the Catholic Daughters of America Poetry Contest.

Luckily, most kids aren't too smart when they rag on you and give you a dumbass nickname. After the poem is published, I'm called names like Shakesqueer and Walt Dickman, but nothing sticks. If you get ragged on with some dopey name and it sticks, that can be your nickname for life, like my friend Billy "Snug" Raines. Back in third grade, we were doing some stupid assignment, another poetry thing, and the teacher asked us if we knew any poems and Billy raised his hand and said, "I'm as snug as a bug in a rug." I didn't think that was so lame, especially for a third grader, but the whole class laughed and from that day on Billy has been known as Snug Raines. It used to make him cry but now he seems OK with it. I guess what choice does he have, right?

So, I get lucky. I didn't get stuck with a dopey nickname after writing my silly poem. Instead, I get a few dead legs, a purple-nurple, and a grandmother who's got me lined up for the priesthood.

5

Something has been going on with my mom. She's down in the dumps almost every day. There's the normal sadness she gets when she talks about her childhood and all the things that are different now, but this summer seems different, and it started even before Pop died. My dad says it's nothing to worry about, that's just the Irish in her.

"We've got no talent for happiness," he says.

I guess the first time I noticed her sadness was a few years ago when I moved out of the room I shared with Tommy because he was hitting puberty and needed his space.

We still had our toys and books and stuffed animals from when we were really little on the dresser shelves and my mom was asking us what we wanted to donate to the poor and what she should box up as a keepsake. As she was standing on a chair, reaching up to take down some stuffed animals from the top shelf, she started crying suddenly. Me and Tommy didn't know what to say, so we said nothing. We just looked down at the floor and hoped she would stop, but she didn't. She just stood there, up on this chair, holding this little stuffed animal bear we called Balboa and cried. When she was done, she spoke.

"I don't know where the years went."

Again, me and Tommy didn't say anything. Then she stepped down off the chair and sat next to me on my bed and handed me Balboa.

"Do you remember when you got this?" she asked.

I shook my head and that made her cry too. She told me that we were having Easter dinner at Grandma from the City's apartment and Tommy had thrown me across the room and I slammed my head on the edge of a desk and we had to go to the hospital to get stitches and that's why I have that scar above my right eye.

"You really don't remember that?"

"No," I say.

"What about you?" she asks Tommy.

"I guess," says Tommy, but he doesn't look up when he says it.

"We ran you down into the car with Grandma and she insisted on taking you all the way across town to Flower-Fifth Avenue Hospital instead of St. Clare's which was only a few blocks away because she worked at Flower-Fifth Avenue and she and I fought the whole way through Central Park because you were bleeding all over me and all over the back seat of the car and your Grandmother kept telling me not to worry, it's just a little blood. You don't remember that at all?"

"No," I say again.

But I've heard this story a thousand times because every Easter we go into the city to go to Mass at Holy Cross on Forty-Second Street where my father and his brother were altar boys, and then we walk over to Tenth Avenue to where my father grew up, and he and his mother tell us all the old stories about hanging out on the stoop and all the trouble he and his brother used to get into, and isn't it a shame that the neighborhood is so dangerous now with these new Irish upstarts that kids can't hang out on stoops all night long and now have to worry about getting stabbed or shot, and my dad jokes that the neighborhood wasn't safe back then and that the only difference was they used to know who the bad guys were. But before we can go up for Easter dinner we have to walk to Thirty-Eighth Street and stand in front of an old garage and Grandma tells how her husband's father, my great-grandfather, was such a great man, a Pioneer, don't you know, and how he took the pledge as a young man to not be a drunk—a "Pioneer" is what they call someone who promises not to drink—and how he started his own trucking company, owned five of his own trucks, and even owned this building we're standing in front of, but his son—her husband, my dad's father, my grandfather—was such a disappointment and a drunk and a fool, that the great man, the Pioneer—the one they called the Big Guy because he was tall as a building and as strong as an ox, whose own father couldn't read or write when he came to this country and yet the Big Guy built his own trucking company—don't you know, he chose not to pass the family business on to a no-good bum of a son, but instead sold it to a friend. We then walk to the Landmark Tavern on Eleventh Avenue and everyone sits at the bar and we toast to all the dead including my grandfather, even though just a minute before we were cursing his name, calling him a louse and a skell if ever there was one who didn't deserve a piece of his father's trucking company because of his wicked drunken ways, but it's Easter and it's a time for forgiveness and that's what you do. Finally we walk back to the apartment at 441 Tenth Avenue, climb the stairs to the fifth floor, and after we have our Easter dinner, Grandma tells the story of when Tommy threw me across the room into the desk and we went to Flower-Fifth Avenue to get stitched up and if we had gone to St. Clare's like your mother wanted to you'd have a much bigger scar because everybody knows the best doctors are at Flower-Fifth Avenue.

I don't remember any of it, but I guess on the way home from the hospital with my eyebrow stitched up, I was still so upset and wouldn't stop crying that we stopped to get ice cream on Third Avenue before going over the Fifty-Ninth Street Bridge and there was the cutest toy store next to the ice cream shop and this little teddy bear was sitting in the window and I begged my mom to get it even though it was pretty expensive and my dad didn't want to because the kid's already got a stuffed animal, doesn't he, and what does he need another one for, but my mom insisted because only that precious cute bear would make her little Kneeney feel better. My dad then insisted we call the bear Balboa because the kid's eye looks like he just went twelve rounds with Apollo Creed and if I have to shell out seven dollars for a stuffed animal he doesn't need then I should at least get the naming rights.

"And the minute you held your little Balboa, you finally stopped crying. You don't remember that at all?" she asks me again and I want to tell her I do remember because I know that's what she wants to hear, but I don't. At that time, I still lived in fear of breaking the Ten Commandments, so I couldn't lie to her.

Then she asks, "So, I'm assuming you want to keep Balboa?"

"No, not really," I say.

Big mistake, I know. That's a time when I'm sure even Jesus woulda said it's OK to lie because she gets so mad at me that she throws Balboa in the garbage can, storms out of the room, and doesn't talk to me for two whole weeks. When my mom gets that pissed, she doesn't say anything, she just gets quiet. "The Queen of the Silent Treatment" my dad calls her.

"Another blessing of an Irish upbringing." He then adds, "As the late Pop McSweeney would say—the rug is there for a reason, so it is."

My dad can tell I don't understand what he means by that. "It's where we sweep all the shit we don't want to talk about."

A few months later when I go up to the attic to get our Christmas lights for the tree, I find Balboa packed up in a cardboard box with all my other childhood stuff. Kinda like the shit under the rug, I guess.

6

Every Fourth of July weekend for the last couple of years we drive out to Montauk to do a father and sons weekend. After the bicentennial, my dad refuses to stay home for the Fourth anymore because every fucking asshole on the block is out there with their bottle rockets and roman candles and if I hear another M-80 go off, I swear to Christ, I'll throw the son of a bitch in jail!

So, we escape the block and go to Montauk instead, which is a beach town at the very end of Long Island. My mom doesn't come with us because she hates fishing and camping, and sometimes she needs a break from us animals anyhow.

As much as I like these trips to Montauk, I'm always a little bummed because I know when I get home, I'm going to hear from my friends all the crazy stuff I missed because somebody always does something stupid in our neighborhood on the Fourth. Like last year, when Frankie McGuiness sent a roman candle flying into the Giordano's garage and started a fire. Or two years ago when the Morans and the Capones got into a fight and started shooting bottle rockets back and forth across the street at each other's houses. Or like three years ago, when the Sullivan kid blew off a few of his fingers lighting an M-80. That was the last straw for my dad, and it was then that he started taking us out to Montauk for the Fourth.

"We don't need to be surrounded by idiots and morons if we can help it." I'm pretty sure he was also afraid my brother Tommy would be right there in the middle of the idiots and morons if we stuck around. "And it's hard to play baseball with two fingers," he told Tommy.

When we go out to Montauk, we always stay at the Hither Hills campground, which is basically just a parking lot, but it's right on the beach. Every family gets a little cement square to set up their camper, but unlike every other family there, we don't have a camper. We just have our tent.

"What are you complaining about? Didn't you say you wanted to live in a tent like the Murphy boys in their driveway?" my dad reminds me.

When we go out there, he likes to wake me up really early and join him for a stroll before anybody else gets up and the beach gets overrun by all the riffraff. Normally on a walk like this we would be laughing and talking, but this summer we were both quiet. Maybe we got too much sun the day before or maybe it was the long drive out there or maybe we didn't get enough sleep because we were up pretty late watching the fireworks, but I don't think it was any of those things. I think it's because we're both thinking about my mom and why she seems so sad. But of course, we don't talk about that, so we just walk in silence and watch the waves break and the seagulls pick at all the trash left on the beach.

The night before, after we set up the tents, we brought our chairs and blankets out to the beach, made a bonfire, cooked some hot dogs, roasted some marshmallows, and watched the fireworks. The town of Montauk does a big Fourth of July celebration where they shoot their fireworks off a barge in the ocean and it's incredible. It's always one of my favorite nights of the summer. When the town's show is done, people on the beach set off their own fireworks, which are always lame by comparison. I don't know why you wouldn't just save them for the next night because they look so small and unimpressive after the big show.

You can probably guess my dad hates the people who light their own fireworks because that's the whole reason we leave our block every Fourth. He also hates people who don't clean up after themselves, and when you walk on the beach the morning after the Fourth, the sand is covered with used roman candles, firecrackers, and bottle rockets. So, as we walk, my dad decides we should collect as much of the trash as we can carry and bring it to one of the metal garbage cans by the dunes. It's pretty early and the garbage trucks haven't come down to the beach yet, so all the trash cans are stuffed to the gills and overflowing, mostly with empty beer bottles and pizza boxes. My dad really can't stand stuff like that, people who leave used fireworks sitting on the beach and dump their beer cans and pizza boxes on the sand when you can clearly see the garbage can is full and you could very easily walk over to the bigger dumpsters in the corner of the parking lot next to the bathrooms.

"Can they really be that lazy? How hard is it to carry your shit another fifty feet to the dumpsters?" he asks.

I nod because I'm not in the mood to get another lecture on laziness which is one of my dad's favorite things to harp on. Anytime I get a bad grade or don't hustle on the basketball court or don't put my dirty socks in the hamper or leave my dishes on the table, he gives me the same line. "You want to know the secret ingredient to becoming a failure? Laziness. And you've got that in spades, kid!" So, I just keep my mouth shut and pick up a few more roman candles.

He can tell I have something on my mind because he gives me one of his looks. And I know what the look means—it means, "What's with the sour puss?"

So, I say, "What?"

"What's eating you?" he asks.

And I know why he's asking. Because I'm not talking and if I'm not talking, he knows I must have something on my mind because usually I'm talking a mile a minute. But I'm too afraid to tell him what I'm thinking so I lie again and say I'm tired. He nods and we walk on, but I think he knows what I want to talk about.

I want to talk about mom. I want to ask him why they don't laugh together like they used to and why does she seem so sad all the time and how come they don't dance to Frank Sinatra in the kitchen anymore and how much more fun would this trip be if she were here with us. But you can't ask your dad that kind of stuff.

If you saw their wedding album you would never believe that they could ever have a fight or that they would ever stop dancing because they looked like these fun silly kids who loved being with each other because they've got these huge smiles on their faces in all the pictures.

Again, he asks me, "You sure you're alright?" And again, I just nod and keep my trap shut and pick up a few cans of Rheingold and carry them to the dumpsters in the parking lot.

Later that afternoon, me and Tommy walk up to Old Montauk Highway to hitch a ride into town. He makes me do the actual hitchhiking since I'm a little kid and more likely to get picked up. Tommy hides in the reeds on the side of the road. I don't know what he's going to do if an old lady in a little two-seater stops for me, but a guy in a pickup truck pulls over and waves me into the back. He doesn't seem to mind when Tommy jumps in behind me. When we get to town, Tommy takes off to score some beer, so I walk around for a while not doing anything, because there isn't much to do. It's a hot summer day and the air is sticky, and everybody is either at the beach or hanging by the pools at all the little motels off the main drag. So I go to Pizza Village and I get a slice and a soda, Welch's Grape—hands down my favorite, even more than Dr. Pepper—and sit on one of the benches outside to have my lunch.

Across the street from the pizza place is the five-and-dime gift shop where we go every summer to pick up a gift for my mom. We've gotten her Montauk towels and snow globes and ashtrays and little lighthouses and toy sharks and a coffee mug that says "Montauk, The End" because Montauk is the very last town on the tip of Long Island. Last year, we got her a T-shirt that says, "I've Got Montauk Sand in My Sneakers." Even though she never comes out here, she loves that shirt and always wears it on Saturdays when she cleans the house and listens to Frank.

So, I'm sitting on the bench eating my pizza and it's actually a pretty good slice—even if my dad says you can't get a decent piece of pizza east of Queens Village—when the lady next to me drops a cigarette on the sidewalk. It hasn't been smoked and musta fallen out of the pack, so I pick it up and hand it to her, but she said, "No thanks honey, you can keep it." So I do.

When I go back into the pizza place to throw my plate and soda can in the trash, because I'm not lazy like "those skells who left all their shit on the beach last night," I grab one of the free books of matches they have on the counter because I've already decided I'm going to smoke the cigarette the lady gave me. Some of my friends have already tried cigarettes and some of the kids in my grade, especially all the girls from Queens, smoke all the time, but I've always been too scared to try it even though my mom and my brother both smoke and my dad smokes cigars and I could sneak a butt at any time because I'm always being sent up to Avalanche's candy store to buy my mom her True Blues and my dad his Te-Amo Relaxations, but for some reason I decide today is the day.

I walk down to the big lake up at the top of Main Street to smoke my first cigarette and think I find a perfect spot where nobody would see me but then I spot this old guy feeding the ducks with his grandkids and I don't want to look like some dirtbag smoking a cigarette in front of these cute little kids feeding ducks, so I keep walking. Every time I think I've found a good spot somebody would come by. Montauk is a summer vacation place and there's tons of people going to the beach or riding bikes and out for jogs so it's tough to find a secret spot. I don't know why I think it's such a big deal, but I want to make sure I'm alone.

Finally after walking toward Hither Hills I find a spot in the cliffs. They got all these little walking paths off Old Montauk Highway where the paths cut through the beach plum bushes and there are sections where the beach plums are so high you end up walking through a tunnel of bushes that lead right to the edge of a cliff that looks out over the ocean. I got to admit, it's a cool spot to have your first smoke. I look around and the coast is clear—get it—so I light the cigarette and take a drag.

I knew I'd hate it because I can't tell you how many times I've been trapped in the car with my mother on a cold winter day and she'd be smoking and the windows would be closed because it was freezing out and I'd be dying to stick my head out for some fresh air. Or even worse was the time that my friend Jimmy's dad drove us home from school when it was raining really bad. Jimmy's dad is not the kind of guy who does stuff with his son, and he is not the kind of dad who drives Jimmy or his friends anywhere, but I guess he made an exception on this day because the storm was pretty nasty. It was one of those thunder showers where the wind is so strong you just know you're going to lose a couple of maples and the next morning you're gonna ride your bike around the neighborhood looking for all the trees that fell over hoping to find one that crashed into a house or on top of a car. Anyway, Jimmy's dad is a chain-smoker and he stubs his butts out on the dashboard of his car so that the plastic on the dash has all these melted cigarette burns. Then, instead of throwing the butts in the ashtray or out the window, he just throws them on the dash that's already covered with hundreds of butts. I think you know what my dad would say if he saw that.

With all the old butts on the dashboard, the reek of Jimmy's dad's car was the worst, even on a summer day with the windows open. Now take that smell and times it by a rainy day where you can't open a window and add Jimmy's dad lighting cigarette after cigarette, and you get the thickest cigarette stank you've ever smelled. To give you an idea of how bad the smell was, I was wearing my Giants winter hat that day, and from then on, we could never get the smell out. It stunk like that car ride for the rest of the winter, even after my mom washed it more than five times.

The reason I'm telling you all this is because you would think with the terrible memory of that car ride and the smell of Jimmy's dad's butts probably still in my Giants hat till this day, that I'd never want to try a cigarette. But I did.

So, I light my first cigarette and do all the tough guy poses I'd seen my brother do. I hold it the way the cool guys on the street corner cup it in their hand. I tried to let it hang out of my mouth like the way Keith Richards does, but the smoke killed my eyes after a few seconds. I pretended to be yelling at some guy and pointing at this imaginary dude with my cigarette held between my thumb and index finger. Finally, after all my posing I took a few drags. I hated it, because if you haven't tried smoking yet, you should know, it really hurts your throat. I finally stubbed my butt out on a rock and flicked it down off the cliffs. My flick was pretty sweet, I have to admit, kinda like the cool guy in that movie, *Breaking Away*, when he flicks his cigarette off the cliffs into the reservoir after he gets pissed that the rich college kid beat him in the swimming race. After my own flick off the cliffs, I start my walk back to the campground.

It's a little too far to walk all the way back, so I decide to hitch and get picked up by some guy with long hair and his girlfriend. When I jump in the back seat, they ask me how old I am.

"I'm gonna be thirteen at the end of the summer," I tell them. "How old are you guys?" I ask.

She says, "I'm nineteen and he's twenty."

That's how old my parents were when they got married but when I look at these two they seem so young. They don't look like adults who could get married and have babies. His eyes are glassy and red and her eyes are pretty and green—like really green—so green that you can't stop looking at them. She also talks real slow when she isn't giggling. They both giggle a lot. She giggles again when he pulls out a roach clip and asks if I want to get high. I say no. He says cool. Then she giggles some more. They look at one another and laugh again and they seem happy. In that moment, they remind me of the pictures in my parents' wedding album. Young silly kids with huge smiles on their faces. So maybe these two could get married and have babies.

I'm only about a mile from Hither Hills when the long-haired guy and his green-eyed girl decide to pull over on the side of the road because he wants to show me the house where the writer E. B. White lives. I've heard of E. B. White because he wrote *Charlotte's Web* and everybody has heard of *Charlotte's Web* even if you didn't have to read it in school because they made a movie out of it. And sure enough, right there on Old Montauk Highway is a mailbox that says E. B. White. The long-haired guy says I should read his other stuff too, even though I never said I read *Charlotte's Web* in the first place.

Long Hair says, "There's a book he wrote called *Here is New York* and when I read that it made me want to move to here. And then I met this Long Island beauty and now I'm staying for good."

That makes Green Eyes giggle again and give him a kiss. This kiss wasn't some short little peck but a full tongue make out. It was weird to sit there and watch them slobbering all over one another. She kept her eyes open and of course I was looking at her and when she saw me watching, she winked. When they finish kissing, Long Hair tells me he's from California and when he got to New York he didn't know that you could surf on Long Island. He thought New York was just the Big Apple. That's what he calls the city, the Big Apple. I think to myself—my dad would hate this yahoo. "Yahoo" is what my dad calls guys with funny accents who aren't from New York who say cornball shit like the "Big Apple." Anyhow, Long Hair loves New York now and will never go back to California because he's got his green-eyed girl and he's found some surprisingly rad waves. Green Eyes loves it when he says this and the two of them start kissing again but now it's less slobbering and more romantic and her eyes are closed and all I'm thinking is I want to get out of the car and walk the rest of the way because it doesn't look like they're ever gonna stop kissing and they're gonna make me late for dinner and then I'll get my ass kicked. Finally, I hop out and start walking and they don't even notice. Only when I get to the gates of the campground do they pass by and honk. Green Eyes blows me a kiss and Long Hair yells, "Remember, *Here is New York!*"

7

The next day we're supposed to do a half-day fluke fishing trip on a party boat leaving from the marina next to Gosman's Dock, but just as we're about to shove off it starts raining. The captain makes an announcement and says we have to sit in the harbor until the storm clears because there's a chance of lightning. Tommy and my dad start fighting because Tommy wants to go home and says he didn't even want to come out to Montauk in the first place and why do I have to do shit I don't want to do when I'm almost old enough to be in the army. And my father tells him because as long as you live under my roof, you'll do as I say. I don't know why my dad forced Tommy to come with us this weekend if he didn't want to. Everyone knows teenagers are moody pains in the asses and if you make them do something they don't want to do all they'll do is piss and moan and sit and sulk and make your life miserable, which is exactly what Tommy has done since we got out here. The three of us sit in silence. The curse of the Irish upbringing. We don't speak, we stew. Finally, I get up and go outside to watch the dark stormy clouds as they head our way from over the ocean.

Outside the cabin is a bench that goes from bow to stern, on both the port and starboard sides, which, if you don't know, is boat lingo for the front of the boat to the back on both sides. My dad taught me that when I was little and every time we go fishing he quizzes me to see if I remember. He also loves to tell me where the word "posh" comes from, not that I've ever heard anybody ever use that word, but if you're curious, it means port out—that's the p-o, and starboard home—the s-h. Got it? P-o-s-h. That was for the rich Brits on their trips back and forth to America. If you were on the left side of the boat, the port side, going to America and on the right side, or starboard side, going back to England, you got to look at the prettier skies on your trip. This explanation would usually then lead my dad into telling the story about our family coming over from Ireland and how when his great-grandfather on his father's side came over they didn't have such choices about what side of the boat their cabins were on because they were dirt poor and starving because of the potato famine and they were stuck crowded with hundreds of other poor Irish peasants in the bottom of the coffin ships for the two-month-long trip and didn't get to see any skies, pretty or otherwise.

He loves talking about all his old Irish relatives and for some reason anytime we go fishing is when he likes to bring them up. His favorite is his grandfather, who everybody called the Big Guy.

"The Big Guy is the one who gave me my love for the sea. Taught me how to fish, how to clam, how to crab. Even taught me how to swim," my dad tells us.

"Oh, I wish you woulda had the chance to meet him. He was the biggest man you ever saw, shoulders as wide as a doorway, which he must have gotten from all that swimming because when he went to the beach, he'd get into the water and swim straight out past the waves and keep going. If he didn't wear this little white sailor's cap you'd think he'd have drowned. But if you looked closely, you could see that little white speck miles out on the horizon and that was the Big Guy."

So, it's because of the Big Guy that we are a beach and fishing family. We have a small motorboat called the "Sea Ya Later." Tommy actually came up with that name when he still participated in family stuff like voting on what we would name our boat. It's a little fifteen-footer with a 55 Evinrude engine that we take into Reynolds Channel to go fluke fishing. The old man obviously loves fluke fishing.

"Just find a good drift, kill the engine, drop your line, hit the bottom, crack a beer and wait."

As we'd wait and drift, my dad would drink his beers while me and Tommy ate our peanut butter and jelly sandwiches, and of course, he would tell us stories about the Big Guy. We'd hear about how poor he was as a kid growing up in Hell's Kitchen with parents who couldn't read or write but how the Big Guy started his own trucking company and how his two sons were such a disappointment to him because they became drunks and half-assed gangsters. This upset the Big Guy so much that he sold the trucking business rather than leave it to the drunken sons, one of which is my father's father, who my dad hated his whole life, and how it's a shame to grow up hating your own father but an even greater shame that you and Tommy couldn't have met the Big Guy because he would have loved you boys because you love fishing, just like he did, but consider yourself lucky you never met your grandfather because he was a no-good skell who got what he had coming.

Those afternoons on the *Sea Ya Later* are my best memories of my brother Tommy because he really does love fishing and when he was on the boat, he was having too good a time to remember to be a dick to me or talk back to our dad. Tommy also likes the stories of the old Irish, but of course, his favorites are the ones about our grandfather, the drunken half-assed gangster skell who my father hated. Before Prohibition, which is when they made alcohol illegal, the Big Guy's regular trucking business was delivering Fleischmann's Vinegar, but when prohibition was going on, he made some extra money on the side delivering booze for a wiseguy named Owney Madden. Owney Madden was some kinda famous bad guy back in those olden times but not so famous that they ever made any movies about him. Anyway, after Prohibition ended, my great-grandfather went back to being a regular truck driver but his two sons, my dad's dad and uncle, continued to work for Owney's gang, "breaking heads and being lowlifes." But that wasn't why my dad hated his father.

"It was because he was a drunk who used to beat me and my mother up every time he got his load on. And he got his load on every day," he told us. "I'd be in bed and I'd hear the asshole stumbling up the stairs of the walk-up in the middle of the night and I'd start praying to Jesus as fast as I could that the old man would trip and fall back down those stairs and break his neck. But that never happened. Then I'd hear him stumbling with his keys at the door, even though we always left the door unlocked because if you had to get out of bed to open the door for him, you'd be sure to get smacked around, and that's when I'd ask the Blessed Mother to please let him just lie on the couch and pass out when he got inside. But that almost never happened either. Instead, he started breaking things, first it might be a glass, then a lamp and then my mother's head. I'd run into the bedroom to try and save her only to be sent flying against the wall with a shot to the jaw."

My dad has these screwed up chipped teeth that were a direct result of "your grandfather's loving touch."

When my dad was in high school, his father was "finally put out of his misery" when he got shot and killed outside the Landmark Tavern on Eleventh Avenue. I only know that because every year on June 6, we go to the Landmark to celebrate, which seems like a sick thing to do but my dad has a sick sense of humor sometimes. The bartender who was working the night my grandfather was killed is called O'D. It's short for something like O'Dwyer or O'Donnell or O'Donoghue and he still works at the Landmark, even though he can barely walk because he's so old now, "but they'll have to carry me out in a pine box to get me from behind this bar, so they will."

O'D has one of those really gruff voices that sounds like he ate a beer bottle and it chewed up his voice box. When I told that to my dad, he laughed and said that it wouldn't surprise him if O'D could eat a beer bottle. After we eat our Landmark burgers and toast to my grandfather's death, and to D-Day, which is also June 6, we go sit at the bar where my dad has a glass of Irish whiskey and O'D tells us the story of how our grandfather was shot and killed. O'D starts by telling us that he hated our grandfather too. He and my dad joke that everybody hated him because he was a typical lowlife skell and nobody likes a lowlife skell and he got what he had coming, so he did.

"A drunk, a degenerate gambler, and a wife beater who owed everybody money. So, you can see why he was adored up and down the Avenue," my father jokes.

On the night of June 6, 1955, one of the shylocks he owed money to came to collect. By the way, a shylock is a guy that lends you money when the banks won't, but unlike the bank, if you can't pay them back, they break your legs or they shoot you, which is what they did to my grandfather.

"I was standing right here, behind the bar, and your grandfather and this particular shylock, who will remain nameless, were arguing, right here where you boys are sitting." O'D says, "I knew your grandfather had been jerking this particular loan shark around for months, so I knew this particular conversation they were having might turn particularly ugly. So, I sent them outside to finish their discussion. And that's when it happened. Right there on that sidewalk there, right outside that window. I can picture it as if it was yesterday."

After telling the part about watching the five bullets rip through my grandfather's chest and the blood spraying onto the window of the bar, O'D then tells us how he quickly kicked everybody out of the joint, locked the door and shut the lights.

"I didn't want the pigs thinking I saw something, and I didn't need them asking me no questions because yous know we don't talk to the pigs around here."

He says this even though he knows my dad is a cop and he's talking to him when he says it. But I guess it's different when the cop you're talking to is there with his sons to toast the death of their grandfather who had five bullets rip through him.

I once asked my dad if he became a cop to find his father's killer.

"Hell no," he said. "Your mother was pregnant and I needed a steady job with benefits."

We go outside to stand above the spot where Grandpa fell

and died. I always get down on my knees and look to see if there is still any blood caked into the cracks of the sidewalk.

"His blood may have washed away, but unfortunately my memory of him won't," my dad says when I can't find a trace of any blood.

"I think it's kinda cool that Grandpa was some badass gangster who got gunned down, right here. I mean, just think about that. He was standing right here, on this spot, when it happened," Tommy says.

"There was nothing cool about it or badass about him. He was just a stupid mean drunk. Remember that," my dad says.

8
—

Speaking of drunks, the day after we got home from Montauk, my mom and Tommy got into a big fight because he came home shitfaced. My mom doesn't ever curse except for the other two times my brother came home drunk and she caught him. He's come home drunk lots of times, but she's only caught him those three times. Talk about breaking your mother's heart. You should have heard her. She was mad and sad in the same moment. I've already decided I'm never gonna drink because I never want to make my mom so mad that she'd start calling me a fucking disgrace and start crying so bad she can barely breathe.

She also caught him smoking pot last week. He was sitting on the roof outside his window so she wouldn't smell the smoke if she walked by his door but he's so dumb, he didn't realize she would smell it if she was in the backyard gardening and that's what happened.

I'm pretty sure Tommy and his friends are becoming burnouts. They all went to Nassau Coliseum in February to see the Pink Floyd concert and ever since then all he does is lock himself in his room and listen to *The Wall* and get high. He only does this when my parents aren't home, except for that day last week when my mom busted him.

When Tommy stumbled through the door last night, my mom was waiting up for him. He could barely walk and she could barely control herself. I mean, she like totally lost it, yelling and screaming and even smacking him one. That's when I woke up.

"I will not have you become a drunk!" she yelled at Tommy. "I've seen it ruin too many lives. People being mean, fighting, driving drunk, getting killed. It leads to no good. Please Tommy, I'm begging you."

I had snuck down and watched them from the top of the stairs. Tommy wasn't even listening to her. He just laughed and lay down on the couch and fell asleep.

The first time Tommy came home drunk, my dad threw me and him in the car and took us down to the Bowery to look at the bums and winos. He said it was good for us to see what happens to you when the drinking gets the best of you. But I could never imagine what these sad smelly dirty guys on the Bowery could possibly have been the best at. Maybe as kids they were good at sports or drawing or playing the piano, but now they just seem lost and lonely. I can remember walking down the middle of the wide sidewalk of the Bowery and the hobos were all sleeping on the curb in the middle of the day, or they were stumbling around talking to themselves or even pissing in their pants. One guy, if you can believe it, took a crap leaning up against a parked car, in broad daylight, right in front of us. It was all pretty sad—for us and for them.

My dad was hoping that seeing the old drunks would scare my older brother Tommy from drinking, but no matter what my parents do to punish him or scare him, nothing seems to work. And it's not just the drinking, it's everything. It seems like every week, Tommy's in trouble for something else.

Last year during Christmas break, my dad even locked me and Tommy in a jail cell at his precinct to warn us about stealing. And another thing, why am I always included in these lessons even if I didn't do anything wrong? Anyway, there weren't any murderers or killers in the jail that day, just a couple of hookers, which if you don't know, are ladies who wear almost no clothes, even in the middle of winter. We saw a few of them that day on the Bowery too, but they weren't nearly as pretty as the girls in the jail cell with us. I'm not sure what they did to get arrested but they weren't mean or scary at all. They were actually really funny. And sweet too. And one of them showed Tommy her boobs. So, I don't think it had the effect on Tommy my dad was hoping it would.

You see, Tommy got in trouble for stealing a *Penthouse* magazine from Avalanche's candy store that year. We call the guy who owns the candy store Avalanche because he's kinda dumb, or at least he seems like he is, since his candy store is the one everybody steals shit from. Avalanche has skinny arms and skinny legs but a huge fat belly and the joke is that the rocks from his head fell into his stomach, like an avalanche. So anyhow, Tommy and his dopey friends went in there to steal a porno mag and thought they had a great plan. They slipped a *Penthouse* into a copy of the *Daily News* and then bought the newspaper and thought they made it home scot-free but Tommy, being the dope that he is, left the dirty magazine sitting on my dad's worktable in our basement. I guess he looks at it when he's down there stealing beers from our basement fridge. When my dad found it, he asked Tommy where he got it. Tommy, of course, lied and said he found it in the garbage, but even I know people don't throw out *Penthouse* magazines because they're even harder to get than *Playboy*s because they show a lot more.

It didn't take long for my dad to find out the truth. First of all, he buys his cigars from Avalanche and is in that store all the time. And it turns out Avalanche isn't as dumb as everybody thinks because he had seen Tommy and the dopes slip the *Penthouse* into the *Daily News* and he figured rather than bust them in the moment, he'd tell my dad the next time he came in there to buy cigars. Which is what he did. Which is how we ended up in the jail cell with the hookers.

"Ironic, ain't it?" Tommy said. "My punishment for stealing a nudie mag was getting to see the real thing in the flesh." I laughed even though I didn't know what ironic meant. Then he called my dad a prick. I didn't laugh at that.

I know I don't want to be like Tommy and I know I don't want to be a drunk. But drinking is one of the things that has me confused this summer because if it's so bad for you why does everybody seem to love it so much. My dad loves beer and all the commercials on TV make it look like fun and all my friends' parents drink and all the teenagers talk about chuggin' and guzzlin' and gettin' wasted and all of that sounds fun too. When I think about my grandfathers it gets even more confusing. My great-grandfather on my dad's side, the Big Guy, took the pledge and became a Pioneer and hated my grandfather for becoming an alcoholic and sold his trucking company to a friend instead of passing it on to that no-good drunk. And my mom's dad, Pop McSweeney, was also a drunk, but not a bad one, or so my dad says.

"Pop was a happy drunk not an angry drunk," he says. "The angry drunk beats his children and beats his wife. Like my father, who was undefeated in every fight he had with my mother. But the happy drunk just dances and sings. But sometimes he falls down the stairs."

On top of being a happy drunk, Pop McSweeney was also a binge drinker which means he won't drink for awhile but then when he does start up drinking again, he disappears, sometimes for weeks at a time and stays drunk the whole time. My mom and her brothers, Mike and Mark, love to tell the story about Pop and his paycheck and his disappearing act. When my mom was little, Pop McSweeney would get his paycheck and take my mom with him on the subway, down from the Bronx to the Emigrant Savings Bank on Forty-Second Street, where he would cash his check. They would then walk over to Third Avenue and go into every Irish bar on the street, where Pop would have a beer, talk to friends, sing a song, and make my mom sit on top of the bar and wait for him. They'd go from one bar to the next, hitting all his favorite "gin mills" until they got to Eighty-Sixth Street.

At that point, he would take what money he had left and give her half and tell her, "Take that home and take care of your brothers and I'll be back in a few days, so I will."

My mom would then climb the stairs to the Eighty-Sixth Street station and get on the Third Avenue El for the lonely ride back home to the Bronx. She'd sit in her seat and peek from the train windows into the apartments along Third Avenue. She'd see families seated around the dinner table laughing and joking, young couples tucking their kids into bed, reading sleepy-time stories, fathers tossing their little boys in the air and mothers dancing with their little girls. She said she wished for a life that looked like those she saw through the windows but more than anything she wished that Pop would make it home that night. But she knew he wouldn't.

Sometimes, he'd be gone for a few weeks and my mother and her brothers would have to take care of themselves which meant getting fed and dressed and off to St. Angela's on their own because if anyone found out their father wasn't home they'd get sent back to the orphanage upstate. You see, my mom and her brothers lived in the St. Joseph's orphanage after their mother died, even though their father was alive, because she died right after their little brother Kevin was born and I guess it was too much for Pop McSweeney to handle raising three little kids and one newborn baby on his own, especially since he only came to America from Ireland a few years earlier and didn't have any relatives to help him. So he gave Kevin up for adoption and put my mom, Mike, and Mark into the orphanage.

My mom says, "He didn't do it because he didn't love us but because he needed to go back to Ireland and find a new wife to help him raise us kids."

He was gone for a few years and didn't find a new bride, so he came back to the Bronx and got the kids out of the orphanage. He tried to raise them on his own for a few years, but it was too hard.

"It's hard for any man to do, let alone a Paddy-off-the-boat with no education and a love of the drink," says my dad.

My mom, Mike, and Mark went back into the orphanage and Pop went back to Ireland again to find a wife. Back then, you didn't fly to Ireland, you had to go by boat. So, when Pop set sail my mom and her brothers had no idea how long he'd be gone.

"Lucky for us, on this trip back to 'the ol' sod,' he found a new wife. My stepmother, Gilligan, whose husband had died a few years earlier, had known my father when they were kids and it was a good fit. Not very romantic but who in this world has time for romance," my mom told us.

When Pop and his new wife Mary Gilligan got back to America they took the three kids out of the orphanage and moved back to the Bronx to an apartment off the Concourse where Gilligan still lives today. I don't call her Gilligan to her face, I call her Grandma, but my dad calls her Gilligan because that's her maiden name. He thinks it's funny because of *Gilligan's Island* and she must think it's funny too because sometimes she'll call Pop "The Skipper" and then all of us will sing, "For a Three Hour Tour" which sounds pretty funny with their Irish brogues.

You can imagine what a tough childhood my mom had, and because of that, anytime me and Tommy complain about how hard something might be—like mowing the lawn, or doing homework, or having to shovel the sidewalk after a snowstorm, she says, "Is it such a difficult life you've had? Would you like your father and I to drop you off at the orphanage instead? You wouldn't last a minute. Now please get to work or we can get in the car and begin our journey upstate."

Even though her father was a drunk and put her and her brothers into the home two different times when he left America to go find a wife, she loved her dad more than she loves anything in the world and if she's ever in a really blue mood and you want to cheer her up, you just have to ask her to tell you a story about Pop McSweeney and she'll start telling you about their train rides into Manhattan with the paycheck, or his singing and dancing and knocking over the living room furniture with his Paddy-off-the-boat friends, or about his crazy dog, Prince, who would follow him to the bar and how this nutty mutt would sit outside and wait for Pop to leave and how embarrassing that would be for my mom because that meant the whole neighborhood knew her father was in the pub in the middle of the afternoon or even worse, first thing in the morning. She laughs about those stories now and all the other stories about the things Pop would do when he was drunk, but she still doesn't want Tommy to drink because even though Pop's stories are funny now, she still wishes she didn't have to take the money at Eighty-Sixth Street and go home on the train without him, looking into the windows on Third Avenue of all of the happy families and pretending her dad was home when he wasn't.

9

I'm still an altar boy and even though I hate it and all of my friends have already quit, my mother is making me stay in the cassocks until I go to high school.

"I still like to see my little Kneeney up there on the altar and it fills me with pride, would you please do it for your mother?" she says. Then she'll put out her arms and ask me to give her a hug and she'll say something like, "I'm gonna lose my little boy soon just like I lost your brother, aren't I?"

And I say, "No, I won't be like him."

But I feel guilty when I say it because I know I'm lying. I mean, I won't be like Tommy, being a jerk all the time and never listening to her and being rude and ignoring her when she tells him to be home for dinner and breaking her heart with his drinking, but I know that's not what she's talking about. She just doesn't want me to grow up, period. And sometimes I don't want to grow up either because it makes me sad because I can feel myself not wanting to hang out with her the way I used to and I always used to love hanging out with my mom.

On rainy days, we would sit at the kitchen table and do puzzles or play gin rummy. On hot summer nights when my dad was working, she would make bowls of popcorn and home-made lemonade with tons of sugar and we would watch TV together. We don't have air conditioning in our house, but we have this big metal fan that sits on the floor in our living room. I would lie on my stomach in front of the fan and my mom would lie next to me and we'd put our faces right up to the spinning blades and sing songs into them and it would make your voice sound funny and we'd both crack up laughing. She also likes to read a lot and she lies on the couch in our living room all day when she's into a good book and sometimes I'll get a comic book and lie there with her, and we'll read for hours, or I'll fall asleep like I used to when I was really little. She loves stuff like that, stuff that reminds her of when I was still her little Kneeney.

My birthday is at the end of the summer, August 31, and it feels like that day is a ticking clock time bomb. I'll be turning thirteen, a teenager, and this worries my mom. She's scared of me growing up and all year has been saying stuff like, "When you turn thirteen you'll turn into a lunatic like every other teenage boy with the hormones and testosterone and my little boy won't want to spend time with me like you used to."

When she says stuff like that, I can see it really makes her sad because she knows it's true, because I don't like doing a lot of the stuff I used to with her because I'm too big now. But I wish I did because I know it would make her happy. So sometimes I force myself to hang out with her but then that makes me even sadder because I see how happy it makes her and then you're filled with guilt on top of your sadness because it would be so easy to do this stuff with her all the time—but still you don't because none of your friends still hang out and play gin rummy with their moms and if you tried to tell them you were staying in to do a puzzle with your mother you'd never hear the end of it and besides, you don't want to be the last momma's boy on Marlboro Road.

So, I decided not to tell her how much I hate being an altar boy because she's down in the dumps enough already without me adding to it. I mean, during the school year, serving Mass isn't so bad because if you have to do a funeral, you get to leave class and walk over to the church during the school day because funerals are usually during the week. And who doesn't mind missing class even if it's because of a funeral. But it's harder during the summer, instead of being outside on a gorgeous day when all your friends are out playing, you're standing on the altar, sweating under your cassock, keeping a close eye on Father Nolan, the priest saying the Mass, because he's always in a bad mood but today he's really pissed off because the other boy you were supposed to serve with, Joey Mullen, didn't show up and if you mess something up—which is what kids do, right?—you know you're getting a smack or worse after Mass.

So now I'm stuck up there alone, kneeling on the sanctuary step and my kneecaps are killing me because Father Nolan doesn't let you use a pad for your knees because he says a little pain in your knees is the least you can do for Jesus considering he took nails to his feet and hands for you and died up there on that cross for your sins, and you want to complain about your knees you little ingrate. But when your knees are hurting, you try to think of something else to forget the pain, and if you get too distracted you might miss the spot during the Eucharistic Prayer when you're supposed to ring the bells and if you mess something up like that—which I did last Sunday—Father

Nolan will make sure to drag you by your ear through the sacristy after Mass to make sure your ears are still working because he can't understand how you couldn't have heard him call the Holy Spirit down upon the gifts and if you're hard of hearing you're not fit to serve his Mass—which is exactly what happened. It's moments like that when you start to wonder why God lets such mean people work for him. But maybe that's what God wants. He wants us to be afraid of him.

I can remember when I was in first grade, and I was just learning how to read, and I picked up the church bulletin to show my dad what a good reader I was becoming but I screwed it up because the bulletin is called "The Good News" but I read it as "The God Knows." My dad started cracking up right in the middle of Mass when I said that.

"The God Knows?" he repeated. "Oh man, they got you shaking in your boots already, don't they?"

On the drive home from church that day him and mom had a big fight over the whole thing.

"You see that's the problem with the church. This poor kid is already afraid of God because he's afraid God knows what he's thinking. Why can't the little guy at least have his thoughts to himself without worrying that whatever weird shit might pop into his head might send him straight to hell?" my dad asks. My mom didn't want to hear it.

She said, "Then he can go to confession and tell the priest all about it and he'll be forgiven."

"But he doesn't need to go to confession because he didn't do anything wrong. And if this crazy vindictive God of ours is all knowing and all seeing, then why does he have to go to confession in the first place? Wouldn't he already know the kid was sorry? And if he did know, would he really care? He's seven years old for Christ's sake."

"Fine," she says. "But when he ends up in eternal damnation let it be on your conscience. And please don't take Jesus's name in vain when you're bashing the church. Two sins don't make a right."

My dad turns to me in the back seat and winks. "Don't worry kid, nobody here is going to hell." Then under his breath, he adds, "Or heaven for that matter."

But my mother hears him and yells, "Don't poison his mind with your blasphemy," and this starts another fight.

I still don't know what he meant by that. Either he thinks there is no heaven or we're all sinners.

My dad was an altar boy when he was a kid, and he says the priests were even worse then. Instead of just smacking you in the back of the head and dragging you by the ear, they'd smack you in the face, with their keys in their hands if you really screwed up, to make sure you really felt it. He served at Holy Cross on Forty-Second Street just off Times Square in Hell's Kitchen. He says the Mass was in Latin back then and that Latin is really hard to understand, so of course you'd never know when you were supposed to ring the bells and then you'd get the keys to the face.

When you become an altar boy, there are initiation rituals the older boys put you through. The priests aren't supposed to know about it, but they must because it usually ends with altar boys crying and what priest doesn't love the sound of that. At our parish, the initiation came during Holy Week when the church would get the delivery of the stacks of palms for

Palm Sunday. Our job would be to separate the palms from the stacks and put them in the boxes to hand out before the Palm Sunday Mass. It was a miserable job because the palms can be really sharp, and you'd get all these little cuts on your fingers. They were like paper cuts, but only worse. The older boys would then take the palms and whip the shit out of the new altar boys. They would aim for your arms and face and neck, anywhere you had skin showing. I had such a big scrape across the front of my neck that I had to tell my mother I got scratched playing Salugi. I knew she'd believe me because any-time you played Salugi, you came home with some kind of scratch, cut, or scrape. If you don't know Salugi, it's like kill the man with the ball, only with two teams. There's no real purpose to the game because there's no way to keep score so it's really just a way to run around and beat the crap out of each other which can be a lot of fun if you're playing with kids your own age. But during lunch recess we usually play our grade against the eighth graders and that always ends with one of the sixth graders crying because some of the eighth graders are already like men with mustaches and muscles and when they tackle you, they really hit you hard. And since we don't have a field at our school, we play in the church parking lot, and it hurts like hell to get tackled on cement. The worst is when they do a pile on and you're stuck at the bottom and you get that feeling like when a big wave keeps you under water and you can't breathe and your heart races and you're screaming for them to get off of you and they just laugh because they're older and when you become a teenager you can't help yourself from being a dick.

When my dad was an altar boy, his initiation was much worse than mine. For some reason, they kept some coffins in the church basement at Holy Cross and the older boys would drag one of these coffins up the steps, put one of the new boys in the coffin, slam it shut and send Holy Cross's newest altar boy flying down the stairs. My dad said when they shut the coffin closed and sent him down the stairs he nearly pissed in his pants and he prayed to Jesus that if he didn't piss himself, he promised he wouldn't do the same thing to the new altar boys when he got older because if he pissed in his pants, the abuse would have been endless. God answered his prayers and my dad didn't piss himself. But of course, when he got older, him and his friends did the same coffin surfing initiation to the younger kids, because that's what older kids do.

10

After dinner on Friday nights, when my dad isn't working, we always go for a walk together at Bay Park. Bay Park is on the bay and not too far from where we keep our boat in East Rockaway. When I was little, me, Tommy, and our dog Kelly would do the walk together but Kelly's dead and Tommy doesn't do father-son stuff anymore because he's too cool to take walks with his dad and his little brother. I have to admit, I miss the walks with the three of us.

When we would pull into the parking lot, me and Tommy would take off immediately and run to the bulkhead where the fishermen would be casting for snappers or crabbing for blue claws. My dad would light his cigar and let Kelly off her leash. Kelly would run off looking for dead horseshoe crabs to do that thing where dogs rub their backs onto any dead creature they can find, which would drive my mom crazy because when we got home, Kelly would jump up onto the couch where my mom would be reading and she would give her a pet but Kelly would have the stink of the dead rotten horseshoe crab on her and then my mom would get the stink on her hand and then she'd yell at my dad who would then yell at me and Tommy to give the dog a bath which Tommy would always make me do by myself. If you don't know, horseshoe crabs aren't the cute little blue claws you get in a restaurant. They're these big brown prehistoric-looking things with an ugly hard shell with little spikes on it and they have a long pointy tail that's poisonous. My dad says they've been around since the dinosaurs, and they look it.

As my dad smoked his cigar and Kelly hunted for a horseshoe crab to roll around on, me and Tommy would head off through the reeds to the water's edge looking for empty beer bottles. When we'd find one, we'd throw it into the water and try to see who could hit it with a rock and sink it first before the current took it out to sea. Even though Tommy always won, I still loved to play that game. It always felt great if a bottle was moving fast in the rip and heading pretty far offshore and you were able to nail it just before it got out of reach.

Bay Park also has a nine-hole golf course, picnic areas, baseball fields, and a giant grass field in the middle of the park where the guys from Jamaica—the country, not the neighborhood in Queens—play cricket. We usually stop and check out the games even if we don't understand what the rules are because it's still fun to watch. One day, when we were younger, me and Tommy were wearing our baseball uniforms because we had just come from our Little League games and the cricket guys asked us if we wanted to try to hit one of their pitches. They let me go first and I whiffed at every pitch but Tommy is a really good baseball player so I knew he would be able to at least make some contact. But he did more than that. Tommy got up there and hit the crap out of the ball and the guys loved it and joked around that he should join their team and Tommy was so happy, he had the biggest smile on his face.

Tommy's always been a natural at sports and sometimes I get jealous because he makes it look so easy. He also makes it look like so much fun because he's always got a huge smile on his face when he's playing. I guess when you're great at something, you smile when you're doing it.

"He's got a hell of an eye, that kid," my dad says as he watches Tommy hit pitch after pitch. My dad was smiling that day too.

But last week it was just me and my dad and he wasn't smiling. Kelly died last summer and my dad doesn't want to get another dog because he says, "I'm not going through that again." By "that" he's talking about when Kelly got sick, and we had to put her to sleep. She had some kind of cancer. Since my mom was too upset and Tommy was who-knows-where, me and my dad took her to the vet to put her down.

My dad didn't want me to go, but I cried and said, "She's my dog and I need to be the last person she sees before she dies so she feels safe." So, my dad let me come with him.

On the drive there, all three of us were quiet. Kelly was quiet and it seemed like she might know what was about to happen. I was quiet because I knew what was about to happen. And my dad was quiet because I think he knew if he tried to talk, he might cry.

You know how sometimes when you're trying to hold back from crying and you're doing a good job and you think you've got it beat but then you have to speak and the minute you open your mouth your chin starts shaking and the floodgates open and the tears start flowing and you're blubbering all over the place? I think that's where my dad was on that drive. And it woulda been a big deal if he started crying because I'd never seen him cry before. Remember he's the guy that makes jokes about his own father getting shot and killed and takes his kids to the bar where it happened so they can toast drinks to celebrate what a great day that was for the family.

When we get to the vet, the doctor explains to us how they're going to put Kelly down. First, they give her one shot that makes her kinda drunk and then the next shot puts her to sleep—forever. I look at my dad as the vet explains this and again, he looks like he's gonna cry any minute. He's getting the thing where your chin starts shaking and you know what happens next. The vet then asks if we want to hold Kelly when he gives her the shots or would we rather wait outside. I want to stay because I want Kelly to see me and feel safe before she goes to heaven.

My dad asks, "Are you sure you want to see that, little guy? It's gonna be pretty sad." These are the first words he's said since we got in the car. But he doesn't look at me when he says them because he can't because the tears are right there just ready to bust out.

I tell him, "I'm sure."

When they give Kelly the first shot, she walks around the floor for a minute and seems normal, like her old self, but then she gets wobbly, like a drunk, three sheets to the wind, and then falls over. I run and pick her up and hold her in my arms and I look to my dad and now it's happened—he's crying.

"Come on, let's leave the doc to it. You don't need to see this."

But I'm not going anywhere. I'm crying now too because I've got Kelly in my arms and I know she's confused but mostly I'm crying because I've never seen my dad cry before and that's making me even sadder.

The vet says, "The boy can stay if he wants. She seems happy in his arms."

My dad can barely talk now with his chin quivering like it is and he just shakes his head and says, "I'll wait for you outside."

My dad leaves and I sit down with Kelly in my arms and the doc says, "I think it's time. Are you ready to say goodbye?"

I nod and kiss Kelly on that spot on her head between her ears where she used to love to get scratched and whisper to her that I love her. The vet takes a needle and sticks it into one of her front legs and when the put-you-to-sleep drug goes in, Kelly turns her head and looks at me, right in the eyes and she looks confused, like she's thinking, "What is going on here?" Then her head just falls over and that's it. She's gone. It was the saddest thing you've ever seen. Even as I write this now, a year later, I'm crying again. The vet let me sit with her on the floor for as long as I want and tells me I'm a strong young man.

"You made that easier for her," he says before he walks out. After a little while, a nurse came in and asked if "we" were OK. I thought that was nice that she said "we." I nodded and she took Kelly from me and a few weeks later we got her ashes. Me and my dad buried half her ashes under the maple tree in our backyard because that was her favorite place to take a pee every morning.

"Now we can never sell this house," I told my dad after we said our prayers. We then took the other half of her ashes and sprinkled them on all the dead horseshoe crabs we could find in Bay Park.

What made Kelly's death and my dad's crying so weird was my dad didn't even seem to like the dog. Once, when we went upstate to the Police Camp for Christmas break, we put Kelly in a kennel. When we got home, me and my mom went to the new Foodtown supermarket to pick up some food for dinner, so my dad went to the kennel to pick up Kelly. He said Kelly seemed normal when he brought her home, but something was clearly wrong with the dog. Usually when my mom's car pulled up, Kelly's ears would prick up and she would go running to the side door to greet her. When my mom would open the door, Kelly would jump up into her arms and lick her face and give her kisses, which my dad always thought was disgusting.

"That dog has been out in the street sniffing ass and eating shit all day and you're gonna kiss that thing," he'd say.

She didn't care. She loved Kelly. But this time, when my mom came home from shopping, Kelly didn't come running. She was hiding under the bed in Tommy's room, of all places, and wouldn't come out. We knew something was off because Kelly never went into Tommy's room because Tommy never paid any attention to her because Tommy was never home. Finally, we had to put a bowl of dog food on the floor to trick her into coming out from under the bed. As Kelly ate her bowl of food, my mom watched her and thought something was wrong.

"Does she look different to you?" she asked.

She did. She looked fatter and shorter and her fur wasn't as shiny. "Yeah. I guess so," I said.

"What the hell were they feeding her in that kennel? Look at her coat. She looks terrible," my mom said.

I got down on the floor to pet her and get a closer look and that's when I saw it. Kelly now had a penis.

"Mom, they did something weird to her. Take a look."

I picked her up to show my mom Kelly's new penis. She

just laughed and shook her head and said it was typical of my father.

"Can you believe that man?" She laughed. "How does he bring home the wrong dog?"

Long story short, me and my mom brought this mangy fleabag back up to the kennel and exchanged him for Kelly. So, you can see why I thought it was weird my dad cried when we put her to sleep.

As me and my dad were walking along the water at Bay Park earlier this summer, I asked him again about getting another dog and again he gave me his same answer that he didn't want to go through "that" again, but he added, "Besides, you're going to be leaving me soon anyhow and that's gonna be hard enough."

"Why would you say that?" I say. "I'm not going anywhere, am I?"

"Yeah," he says, "It'll soon be time to leave the nest just like your brother Tommy did."

I act like I don't know what he's talking about but of course I do. It's the exact same thing my mom is afraid of. Teenagers break up with their parents and it makes their parents sad. When Tommy became a teenager, he dropped my parents like a bad habit. He stopped wanting to go fishing, and to the beach, and to the movies, and never wanted to sit in the backyard on a summer night and watch the Yankee games—all the stuff we used to do together as a family.

"Look, it's what happens when you hit puberty. It's natural. You're gonna want your independence. And hanging out with your old man isn't gonna be cool. Besides, once the hormones kick in, you're gonna become a mean, moody prick like your brother and I'm not gonna want to hang out with you anyhow." He tries to make a joke of it because that's what he does but I know he doesn't think it's funny.

Now I feel my chin shaking and the tears forming in my eyes and I can't stop them because I'm afraid it's true because I watched it happen with Tommy. Tommy would yell and scream at my dad, and it would make me so sad when they were fighting that I swore to myself I would never be like that. I give my dad a hug to hide my face and my tears, and I tell him I'll never leave him. But I'm afraid. My birthday is coming up at the end of the summer and I'll be a teenager then and the hormones will kick in and puberty will hit, and I'll become moody and sour-pussed and I know it's impossible to control these things because I've never met a teenager who isn't a jerk to his parents.

When he sits on a bench to finish his cigar and watch the fishing boats come back to their marinas, I come up behind him and wrap my arms around his neck and rest my chin on his shoulder to watch the boats with him.

He tells me, "This right here, kid. This is what I'll miss the most."

His voice sounds weird, it's soft in a way that it never is, and I can't look at him because I know he's crying again, and I don't want to see it.

Later when I got home, I try to tell Tommy about the weird conversation with dad and the tears and he just says, "Fuck him. Dad is a pain in the ass."

11

Last year for my birthday my dad got me a typewriter. That's what happens when you win a poetry contest. Lucky me. My dad made a big deal of the whole thing, presenting this type-writer to me like it was a new bicycle or something. It isn't a new electric typewriter or anything fancy, he just fixed up this big old black metal thing we had buried with the rest of the junk in the basement. He said it was his father's.

"Not that the asshole could type. The bum could barely read."

"So why did he have a typewriter?" I ask.

"Because, for a short time, your grandfather was a salesman for the L. C. Smith Typewriter Company until he got fired for stealing some of his inventory and selling them out of the trunk of his car," my dad says. He worked there during World War II so you can imagine how old this thing is, but so far, it still works.

"For some reason, he held on to this one and when Grandma finally cleared out his closet, she found it hidden on the top shelf under seven old shoeboxes filled with five and ten dollar bills," he said.

As happy as I am with the typewriter, I would have preferred the shoeboxes filled with money.

"Why did he keep all that money in shoeboxes instead of the bank?" I wanted to know.

"Your grandfather was convinced the world was full of crooks and that included the banks," my dad said. "Takes one to know one he would say."

"What did Grandma do with all that money?" I asked him.

"She gave me two grand to help put a down payment down on this house. So, in the end, I guess the old son of a bitch actually did do something for me," he jokes. "And now with this typewriter he's done something for you too."

My dad loves telling us our family's New York history. He's taken me and Tommy to every building that every relative of ours has lived in or worked at, including the old L. C. Smith Typewriter Company's office on Broadway near City Hall and the Woolworth Building. We've been to the old Nabisco factory on the West Side Highway where his mother worked during the war, his grandfather's trucking garage on West Thirty-Eighth Street, the tenement at 441 Tenth Avenue where my father was born, the old stables on Twenty-Eighth Street, which is now a taxi repair shop, where his great-grandfather was a stable boy in the 1880s, and the rooming house on Eighth Avenue where that same great-grandfather met his wife, my great-great-grandmother. We've been to all the churches, like St. Bernard's on Fourteenth Street where his parents were married and Holy Cross in Times Square where he was an altar boy and rode the casket down the church basement stairs. We've been to the block where his old high school, St. Ann's, used to stand on Seventy-Sixth and Lex, before they knocked the building down and moved the school to Queens. When we stood on the sidewalk where the front steps of his old school used to be, my dad shook his head and recited this poem he loves:

"I've walked this block before, it's name is still the same;

I'd left for just a while, yet none of my past remains;

This city forever changes, it's streets and spirit are free;

Not mine to own, not mine alone, New York moves on without me."

I don't want you to think that since I won a poetry contest I now memorize poems as well and can just spit them out like my dad can. I had to go downstairs to the basement workroom and copy it off this framed black-and-white photograph we have. It's a picture of the old Penn Station and the poem is on that. If you really want to see my mother cry, just ask her about the old Penn Station.

We've also been to every precinct my dad has worked in, the 2-4 on the Upper West Side, the 6th in Greenwich Village, the 19th on the East Side, the new Police Headquarters down near City Hall, and the old Police Headquarters, which is my favorite of all the old buildings in the city. When we went there, my dad showed us the corner window on Centre Street that used to be Teddy Roosevelt's office when he was the Police Commissioner. He showed us the back door on Baxter Street that led down to the jail cells. He described how sometimes the bad guys would make one last attempt to escape when the cops would take them out of the paddy wagon, and he'd have to chase them up the block. He laughed when he said paddy wagon and warned me never to repeat those words in front of Pop McSweeney because my mom's father hated that term.

Pop would say, "It's anti-Irish, so it is. Paddy wagon, a wagon for Paddys, is it? It certainly is and that's anti-Irish!"

He had a list of other words he said "that are all tossed about at the Irish's expense. Hooligans, shenanigans, donnybrook, and mulligan to name a few. And I will not stand for any anti-Irish sentiment in this house, so I won't."

Pop ended all his sentences with something like, "So I won't" or "So it is" or "So I do." Like when we went to his apartment and Tommy stole a bottle of beer to drink on the roof, he said, "I want to know which one of you two blaggards stole my last bottle of Schaefer's, so I do."

When my mom found out we'd been to where my father's high school was, she got upset that my dad didn't take us down to her high school.

"Just a few blocks down Lexington Avenue wouldn't have been so hard, would it?" she said.

So we had to make a special trip into the city to see her high school as well, St. Vincent Ferrer, on Sixty-Fifth and Lex, which is a block from Donohue's Tavern, which is where we go every St. Patrick's Day after the parade because we know the owner, Mike, because it's right down the block from the 19th Precinct where my dad used to work. Donohue's is also where my mom had her first legal drink after she and her classmates turned eighteen and where her father took her for dinner to celebrate after her high school graduation since it's just a few doors down from the school, so it is, and wouldn't it be grand to stop in and celebrate with a drink.

Donohue's holds a lot of memories for my mom. On St. Patrick's Day, my mom will make sure she has one drink at the corner of the bar by the front window, so she can toast to her old girlfriends and their high school days.

"I can remember sitting with my friends, right here on these stools, like it was yesterday," she tells me. "We raised our drinks and toasted to our big plans for the future. And now the future is here, and it all went by too quickly," she adds with the sadness in her eyes.

It was in that same corner of the bar last St. Patrick's Day when I first realized that maybe my parents weren't so happy together. My mom was talking to the wife of another cop, but she didn't realize I was standing next to her listening in.

"When he told me he was joining the cops I can remember thinking, 'Well, there goes that dream,'" my mom said.

"What dream was that?" asked the lady.

"That I'd have the kind of life that was different from the one I grew up with. You know, just making ends meet. A civil servant's wife, living paycheck to paycheck."

"Oh, it's not so bad," said the lady.

"No. But it's not the life a young girl dreams of, is it?" asked my mom.

I turned away quickly and ran back through the crowd to find some other kids who were sitting under a table sharing a beer they stole off the bar. I took a sip so they wouldn't make fun of me and then took another sip because I was sad and all the sad people I know drink, especially on St. Patrick's Day. And even though I took the sips under the table that night I'm not going to be a drunk who breaks their mother's heart, but on that Paddy's Day, I didn't care about her heart.

12

I was down in the basement listening to a Rolling Stones album when my mom came walking through with the laundry. Our laundry room is down in the basement next to the boiler and across from my dad's workroom. He calls it his workroom even though he doesn't really do any work down there. It's just where he keeps all his tools and a bunch of coffee cans filled with loose nuts and bolts and his *National Geographic* magazine collection. He's got a bookshelf down there that covers the whole wall and it's filled with hundreds of *National Geographics* going back to even before he was married. I don't know why he still keeps them because it's not like he ever reads the old copies and it's not like me or Tommy are ever going to read them. Although Tommy has a few he keeps hidden under the basement sink that I'm not allowed to look at or tell mom and dad about because if you do it'll be the last thing you fucking do, you hear me, you dumb little shit.

Tommy also keeps his weights and workout bench down in the workroom and he has a speed bag hanging on the ceiling. When he's working out on that thing you can hear it rat-a-tat-tatting up through the whole house and it drives my mother crazy because first of all, it sounds like machine gun fire when he gets a good rhythm going and second of all, if he's working out he's gonna be blasting some "getting pumped" music like Zeppelin or AC/DC and he'll have it cranked to ten and my mother can barely hear herself think and wouldn't it be nice to have some peace and quiet in this house on the weekends.

This is why I've got the Stones playing at a respectable level so when she walks through with the laundry she just smiles and nods at me. The Rolling Stones are my favorite group by far and I've got my neighbor from up the block, Sonny, to thank for that. You see, a few years ago, Sonny fell in love with disco and decided rock and roll was dead, so last summer he held a garage sale on his front stoop to finally get rid of all his old rock albums. He had two milk crates filled with all his old records and he was selling each album for two dollars. I ran home and scrounged five bucks from my piggy bank and some loose change I found around the house so I was only gonna be able to buy two records but Louie had six dollars so he was getting three. As we each start going through the milk crates, Louie quickly found Yes's *Fragile*, The Who's *Who's Next*, and Billy Joel's *The Stranger*, and I'm pissed because there's nothing good in my crate until I find the Rolling Stones's *Hot Rocks* but it's a double album and Sonny wants $3.25 for the double albums so if I want the Stones I'm not gonna be able to get another record. So I tell him I've only got five bucks on me and could he maybe cut me a break on a second record and he says sure, but he says he gets to pick it since he's losing money on the deal and I say OK. He offers me Neil Young's *Live Rust* which is also a double album, because Sonny says he hates Neil Young and he hates live albums and he adds, "Besides, Neil Young doesn't know what he's talking about when he says rock and roll will never die because it's already fucking dead" and he's happy just to get rid of it. So, he gives me *Live Rust* for a discounted price of $1.75. So now I've got four actual vinyls for my five bucks, which pissed Louie off because he only got three for his six bucks.

That night I took the albums down to the basement where we keep Tommy's old record player. When Tommy got a new stereo for his sixteenth birthday, my father moved his old one down here because in our house we don't throw anything out. We either put our old shit down in the basement or up in the attic. Almost every inch of both floors is covered with stuff most families would throw out or give to the Salvation Army, but not us. I already told you about all the old *National Geographic* and that's just the start of it. We got lamps, tables, chairs, two old couches, sports equipment, pots and pans, you name it, we got it, as far as the eye can see.

"If I paid good money for something, why would I ever throw it out?" my dad asks. So that means, if he bought something and it entered our house, it was never ever gonna leave. We've got boxes piled on top of crates that are stacked on top of shelves going all the way to the ceiling. Even the bar in the basement is cluttered, covered and stacked up with all this old crap.

That's right, we have a bar in our basement. That's a weird thing about our neighborhood, all the houses have tavern style bars built into their basements. Mr. Ford told my dad that when Mr. Gibson built these houses in the 1920s it was during Prohibition so he figured people who wanted to drink would have to do it in their own home.

Most people don't use their bars except for Louie's and my friend T-Mac's families. Louie's dad is a handyman and is always redoing bathrooms and kitchens or fixing windows and doors or painting ceilings and waxing floors, so he turned their basement into a German beer hall, or at least that's what Louie's dad calls it. It's actually pretty fancy so we're never allowed to go down there. T-Mac's dad is a mailman so theirs isn't as fancy. But T-Mac's family is always throwing parties in their basement bar and his older brothers are allowed to hang out down there and drink, even though they are only sixteen and seventeen. T-Mac says we'll be allowed to go down to drink once we get into tenth grade but like I already said, I'm not gonna be a drinker who goes and breaks their mother's heart.

Tommy, who doesn't care about the heartbreak of our mother, asked my dad to finish our basement and fix up the bar so we could use it for parties, but my dad says, "Who the hell would want to drink in their basement when there's so many good bars in the world." So, it's on top of our unfinished bar that I found Tommy's old record player buried under some old shoulder pads and a football helmet.

The reason I was down in the basement with my new Stones and Neil Young albums, digging out Tommy's old record player is because I don't have my own, although that's what I want for my thirteenth birthday. I never used to listen to any music other than what my parents were playing in the car or what my mom listened to when she was cleaning the house on Saturdays and when she's cleaning on Saturdays, she's only got ears for Frank. In the car we usually listen to WABC and they play whatever the big hits are at the time. Like this summer, that sad song "Sailing" is on the radio anytime we go anywhere.

Tommy says it sucks and only a real pussy would like a song like that, but I have to admit I dig it. So does my mom. Me and her have that in common, we both like sad songs. But before getting *Hot Rocks* and *Live Rust*, I never had any music that I really cared about. I have a little transistor radio, you know the ones with a strap for your wrist, that I hang on my bedpost but all I ever used to listen to were the Yankee and Knick games and sometimes Jean Shepherd on the nights my mom kicked me out of her bed. But that night in the basement last summer, everything changed.

I decide to listen to *Hot Rocks* first since unlike Neil Young, I had at least heard of the Rolling Stones, but I didn't really recognize any of the song titles other than "Satisfaction" and "Jumpin' Jack Flash." So, I started with side one of the second album because "Jumpin' Jack Flash" is the first song on it and the next song was called "Street Fighting Man" and I figured that must be cool.

From the moment I dropped the needle down, I became a Stones fanatic. I sat down there all night long listening to side one over and over and over again. "Jumpin' Jack Flash," "Street Fighting Man," "Sympathy for the Devil," "Honky Tonk Women," and "Gimme Shelter." A year later, older and wiser, I know how lucky I was that those five songs were my introduction to rock and roll.

Anyway, I was down in the basement again, by myself, lying on one of the two old couches, which is where Tommy used to make out with his girlfriend every night before they broke up because he's not allowed to bring girls up to his bedroom because we're not running a house of ill repute for you and some hussy to do as you please. I'm playing side one of *Hot*

Rocks over and over again and it's making me want to cry. Side one has some really sad songs like "Play with Fire" and "As Tears Go By" and when Mick sings "Smiling faces I can see, but not for me," I nearly lose it. So maybe I've got a little bit of my mom's sadness in me because why else would I listen to these depressing songs over and over again when I know they're gonna make me cry. And then, right as I'm thinking that, my mom steps out of the laundry room and wants to know the name of the song that was just playing and I tell her it's called "As Tears Go By."

She asks me to play the song again and I get up and move the needle back. She then sits down next to me on the couch. She doesn't say anything while we listen to the song and I don't say anything either. We just sit and listen, and she starts crying but I still don't say anything because what are you going to say when your mom is crying to a Rolling Stones song. Talk about a sad night on Marlboro Road.

When "As Tears Go By" ends she wipes the tears from her eyes and says that was a nice song and gets up and goes back to the laundry room. I know something's wrong because your mom shouldn't just sit next to you, listen to the Stones, and cry. It's like earlier in the summer with my dad at Bay Park when I put my arms around his shoulders as he sat on the bench and watched the fishing boats come back to their marinas and I could tell he was crying. I know I don't know much but I do know parents shouldn't cry in front of their kids unless they're at a funeral because it's way too confusing and just plain scary to think about.

Two songs later, "Mother's Little Helper" comes on and she comes out again, but now she's carrying the laundry basket, and she says, "Mother's little helper? That's what I could use." Then she laughs as she heads up the basement stairs. I don't really know what she means by that or why she laughs, but it seems like everything must be OK now.

After she goes upstairs I play "Mother's Little Helper" again but this time I really pay attention to the lyrics. There's a line in there about the mother burning her frozen steak and I figure that's what she's talking about, because she's not really the best cook, but then it gets to the line about the overdose and that's when I realize the song is about drugs. So now I'm really confused. Was my mother saying she wants or needs to take drugs to help her through her busy day?

That night after we ate, she was sitting on the couch reading like she does every night after dinner and as I headed out to go see who was hanging on the block, she stops me and holds up her book and says, "This is my mother's little helper."

13

I've been staying up pretty late typing away and my mom says she's having a hard enough time falling asleep without hearing my clackity-clack at one in the morning.

"And why don't you go to bed already and what is it you're writing anyway? *War and Peace?*"

I shrug and pull the page out of the typewriter and shove it in my desk drawer because I really don't want her to read it, especially the stuff where I talk about her being so sad and crying.

"What's wrong? You don't want me to read it?"

"I'd rather you didn't," I say.

"Why not? Are there some things in there you don't want me to know?" I shrug. Then she looks at the stack of all my typed pages on my desk and she puts her hand on it as if she's going to pick up the first page and read it anyway, even though I told her I didn't want her to.

"Has your father read it?"

"No," I tell her.

"OK, I understand," she says. I know her feelings are hurt, and I wish I could let her read some of the pages, but I know if she reads the wrong section she'll get upset and I don't want to add to the sadness.

One day, when she got home from work, she came into my room again, only this time she was carrying a bunch of books she thinks I need to read.

"If you're going to be a writer, you might want to read these. They're some of my favorites and they all happen to be Irish Americans."

I nod and hope she isn't really expecting me to read all these books because they look really hard and boring.

She left the stack of books on my desk and went down to the kitchen to make dinner. I looked at the books and never heard of any of them except *The Old Man and the Sea* because I saw some of that movie one night when there was nothing else to watch on TV. The other books were *The Great Gatsby* by a guy named Fitzgerald—which is actually my dad's mother's maiden name and my middle name, so maybe I'll look at that one—and the complete works of Eugene O'Neill. Looking at the titles, the O'Neill books look really boring except maybe *The Hairy Ape*. But *Long Day's Journey into Night* sounds like a tagline for the most boring story ever told.

I don't know if I mentioned this but I'm not really much of a reader and it drives my parents crazy because both of them read all the time and they can't understand why I don't just sit with them on the couch or on our towel at the beach and disappear into a good book. What can I say? I'd rather play than disappear.

When I come down for dinner, it's just me and my mom because who the hell knows where Tommy is and my dad's working. She knows if it's just the two of us she doesn't have to make a whole big meal, so it's a tuna fish sandwich for her and liverwurst and baloney for me.

"I still don't understand how you and your father can eat that crap," she says. "That's not even meat. I don't know what it is."

I tell her we eat it because it's delicious. "Like the dirty water hot dogs we get in the city," I say.

"You're your father's son," she says, and I can see the sadness coming into her eyes when she says that, so I quickly change the subject.

"Where's Tommy?" I ask.

"Who knows?" she says, and this makes her sadder and madder than she's already been, and I realize that was a stupid thing to ask, so I don't say anything else. I just focus on my liverwurst and baloney sandwich.

I guess now would be a good time to tell you more about my brother Tommy. You see, it wasn't always so bad between him and my parents. I mean, he used to be their favorite. He was the firstborn son and in an Irish house, that child holds a special place, so he does—or at least that's what I overheard Pop McSweeney say once. But now God's gift is always in trouble, so he is. And it all started when he decided to leave Chaminade.

Chaminade is an all-boys Catholic high school that Tommy went to for his freshman and sophomore years, but then left to join his neighborhood friends at the public school. The main reason Tommy went to Chaminade was to play baseball because he used to think he was gonna be some kinda big baseball star and play in the majors, but when he got there something like 120 kids tried out for the freshman team and Tommy didn't make the cut because he was a late bloomer and hadn't really hit puberty by then, so he was still pretty short and skinny. But Tommy's one of those kids that does the thing he says he's gonna do and he said he was gonna be a baseball star so he was gonna do whatever it took to make that happen. My dad jokes that the first word that little baby Tommy ever said was "determined." He said it after he climbed up and outta his crib for the first time—or so the story goes. So, Tommy worked out that whole summer before tenth grade to make the JV team.

"Ass up, head down, Tommy!" That's what my dad would tell him. I think that means work hard and don't think too much about it. But Tommy would get discouraged sometimes because even with all the hard work, he wasn't getting any bigger.

"Don't worry about that. Just like the hair on your balls, it's gonna come. It's just gonna come a little later for you than the other kids. It's the Hibernian Curve," my dad would tell him. I'm not quite sure what the Hibernian Curve is, but it seems to be connected to Irish kids and when they grow hair on their balls.

My dad and Tommy were best friends that summer, lifting weights and going jogging and watching Yankee games in the backyard. My dad would take the small black-and-white TV from his bedroom and run an extension cord out the kitchen window so he and Tommy could watch the game while my dad smoked his cigar as they discussed every play. Then over the winter, Tommy finally got his growth spurt and got really big and strong, and when spring came he made the JV and my dad was so proud.

"What did I tell you Tommy Boy, hard work pays off. Just put in the work and good things will come," my dad told him.

But then in the third game Tommy broke his arm sliding into home and had to sit out the rest of the season and he got really depressed and decided he hates Chaminade and at the end of the school year he told my parents he wanted to leave so he could go to the public school in town with all his buddies. My dad hates Tommy's dopey friends, and he was afraid that if he went to the public school with them, they were going to be a bad influence on him.

"Your dopey friends are morons and idiots and if you hang out with morons and idiots you become a moron and an idiot."

Tommy didn't care. He was done with Chaminade and that broke my parents' hearts because they really wanted Tommy to graduate from there so he could get into a good college because neither one of them went to college and he would have been the first in our family with a college degree but now Tommy seems to have turned into a moron and idiot just like his friends and none of those dopes are going to college and you're only as good as the company you keep and what the hell are you going to do with your life now.

14

I missed my baseball game tonight because of Pop's wake. The reason we're still playing in July when all the other Little League seasons have ended is because those leagues are for rich kids who go to summer camp in July and August. We joke that our summer camp is Marlboro Road and it's a lot more fun than hiking through the woods or paddling a friggin' canoe.

I love it when we have our baseball games during the week because those are usually night games, and we play under the lights and it's obviously cooler out once the sun goes down. On the weekends you could have a game at eight in the morning and nobody wants to do anything at that hour other than watch TV, or you could have a game at noon, in the middle of August, when it's a thousand degrees out and it's so humid and sticky, and the sun is so bright that you don't even want to play baseball, which is something you can't even imagine thinking when you're sitting in school on a snowy day in February.

You got to understand, me and my friends are obsessed with baseball and play every form of baseball you can think of. Stoopball, whiffle ball, and stickball are the most popular because you can play any of those with just a few kids because you play automatics, and you don't need to run the bases, so you don't need all those fielders. Automatics, if you don't know, are when you pick a spot on the street like a sewer cap or a parked car or a tree or a fire hydrant and if you hit the ball past that spot, it tells you what your hit is. Like if I hit it past the sewer cap in front of the Horowitz's house, it's a double, and if you hit it past the Kids at Play sign on the telephone pole, it's a triple, and if one goes all the way past the Lincoln Continental parked in Tony Cazuba's driveway, it's a homer. If we're playing stoopball, we use the house across the street for our automatics. If you hit it into their bushes, it's a double. If you hit below the second story windows, it's a triple. If you hit it above the windows, it's a homer. If you hit one that breaks a window, it's time to run like hell.

My house sits on the corner of Marlboro Road and Page Road. We call that intersection Four Corner Stadium because we use the four corners as our baseball diamond. We only use bases when we get a bunch of other kids from the neighborhood for a bigger game. If we're really lucky we can sometimes play nine-on-nine but it's usually four-on-four. If we don't have enough kids for a pitcher, you have to self-hit, which is when you're batting, you toss the ball up to yourself and swing. The games we put together at Four Corner Stadium are our favorites because it feels a lot more like real baseball with the base running and double plays and tagging up. We use my house's corner as home base and the other three corners as first, second, and third. The house on the second base corner is owned by Mrs. Jansen and we use her front lawn as center field. She's another one of the old biddy early settlers but she never comes out of her house. The only time you ever see her is when she takes a bucket of water—we hope it's just water—and tries to dump it from the second story window down onto whoever is playing center field. She's also got a side yard with one of the biggest old maple trees on the block, but it's covered in ivy and the ivy covers the whole side yard too, so if you hit the ball in there, it's a ground rule double because it can take you over an hour to find it. When you're digging through the ivy, we have to keep one kid on lookout because that's usually the perfect time for Mrs. Jensen to dump her bucket of who-knows-what on you because you're a sitting duck right under her window.

We also lose a lot of balls down the sewer. There's a sewer grate on my corner so if there is a play at the plate and it's a bad throw the ball can disappear down there. I know it seems like something that wouldn't happen that much, but you can't believe how many balls we lose down the sewer every summer. If we haven't had any rain in a while, my friend Mark will stick his hand down there to find it because he's tallest of all of us and his arms are long enough to reach for the balls but he doesn't like to do it because he swears that one time he got bit by a rat but none of us remember that. If my dad is home, he'll get his crowbar and pop off the sewer cap on the sidewalk and scoop out all the balls with his fishing net. If we've had rain, the balls are all floating down there along with everything else that washes down from the street and it's pretty disgusting. So even if we do fish a few balls out of there, you can't continue to play because the balls are soaking wet and stink like sewer water, especially the tennis balls, so you have to chuck them in a bucket with soap and then let them dry out in the sun for a day or so. If that happens and we're in the middle of a game and we still want to play, we have to ride up to the country club and dig through the bushes behind the tennis courts to find some new balls that the rich people were too lazy to look for.

Anyway, the reason we play our Little League weekday games at night is because it's a dads coaching league and the dads need to get home from work before they can coach. The night games are also so much more fun than the day games because the bleachers are packed with everybody's parents and brothers and sisters showing up and there's nothing better than hearing the crowd cheer after you make a diving catch or you drive one up the middle to score the winning run. Although sometimes the crowd can get a little rowdy. It's usually when somebody's dad has brought a few six packs to the game and the ump calls their kid out on a close play or the kid goes down looking and the six-pack dad doesn't like the call so he starts cursing at the ump and another dad from the other team starts yelling at him to shut the hell up and let the ump do his job and before you know it, you got two dads throwing punches in the parking lot.

I'm not nearly as good a baseball player as my brother Tommy. Tommy says it's because I'm afraid of the ball. I tell him I'm allowed to be afraid of the ball because I've had my nose broken two different times playing baseball. The first time was when I was playing first base against the Blessed Sacrament Fireballs. You should know our league has weird names like that. Instead of being called the Yankees or the Mets or the Giants like most other Little Leagues, our teams are named after churches, lodges, and neighborhood associations. My team is the Gibson Road-runners and Tommy was on the Gibson Lions because our teams are sponsored by the Gibson Civic Association. Last week we played the Police Boys Club Shields, the week before we played the VFW Minutemen, and tonight we play the American Legion Blue Jackets. It kinda stinks that we have these weird team names because that means we also have these weird, lame uniforms and hats, unlike the kids who play in the other Little Leagues who have cool uniforms that look like the uniforms in the Major Leagues.

So let me tell you how I broke my nose the first time. There were two outs in the bottom of the seventh—we only play seven innings in Little League—and the other team, the Blessed Sacrament Deacons, had the winning run on third. I was playing first and this kid on Blessed Sacrament hit the cheap little grounder to our shortstop, Geezer. We call him Geezer because he sounds like a wise old man when he talks. Like when we complain about the batting order, he says things like, "Ours is not to reason why, ours is to do or die!" You never know what Geezer is talking about. So Geezer rushes this little cheapo, bare hands it and whips it over to me with this crazy sidearm motion he's got and I put out my glove, ready for the ball, and I can see it coming at me but this kid on Blessed Sacrament must be some kind of speed demon because he's booking down the first baseline and it's gonna be a close play. At the last second, I do something very stupid. I look to the speed demon and take my eye off the ball, which you should never do, because if you take your eye off the ball, you might get hit right in the friggin' nose. Which is exactly what happened to me on that play. Bam. Crack. Crunch. Right on impact my nose turned into a faucet and the blood flowed all over my uniform. Not that I really cared since our uniforms are so lame to begin with, but what really sucked is the kid was safe at first which allowed the kid on third to score which is how we lost the game. Sitting on the bleachers afterwards with a bunch of tissue paper stuffed up my nose, Geezer said, "That was the very definition of adding insult to injury." See what I'm saying about Geezer. What kid talks like that?

The second time I broke my nose was last year. Coach had moved me over to third base, the hot corner, but we soon discovered I'm not a very good third baseman either. In one game, I had two different ground balls go right through my legs and roll out to the outfield. This happened because I committed the two cardinal sins of playing the infield. I didn't get my glove down all the way to the dirt and again, I took my eye off the ball. But this time, it wasn't to look at a base runner, it was because the ball was coming at me so fast, I turned my head away because I was afraid of breaking my nose again. After that game I was pretty embarrassed because you don't want to be the kid who lets not one but two balls roll through your legs. On the drive home my dad asked me if I still wanted to play baseball.

"Of course I want to play. I love baseball," I said.

"Then you're going to have to get over your fear of the ball. You think you can do that?"

"Yeah, I guess."

"You guess, or you know?"

"I know?"

"Is that a question or an answer?"

"An answer," I say.

"OK then. That's what we'll do," he said. I could already tell this was gonna end badly.

We went up to the high school baseball field and my dad

stood me against the backstop and started hitting grounders at me, forcing me to keep my eye on the ball and getting my glove down.

"I'm gonna hit one a little harder," he said, and he took a step closer as he swung. The ball took a wicked hop off a rock and bounced up and hit me in the shoulder.

"Did that kill you?" my dad asked.

"No," I said. But it did hurt like hell.

"See," he said, "No need to be afraid of the ball."

He kept hitting the ball harder and harder and moving in closer and closer and I was doing great. I looked like Graig Nettles out there, scooping up everything he was hitting at me until one ball came off the bat in a line drive. I never saw it coming because I had been looking down into the dirt in front of me for so long, keeping my eyes glued to the ground, that I never expected a line drive. My dad didn't expect it either.

"The minute that ball left the bat, I thought to myself, 'Oh shit, he's a dead man,'" he told Tommy and my mom at dinner that night. "The poor kid is looking down expecting another grounder and here comes this rocket headed right for his kisser. He never had a chance."

Tommy laughed. My mom scowled.

"I tried to warn him but it was too late. A second later, he's down on the ground, blood gushing out of his nose, screaming and crying."

"I hope you're proud of yourself!" My mother yelled at my father.

"What are you going to do?" my dad said. "It happens. Everybody gets their nose broken at some point."

I wanted to remind him that I already had my nose broken

once before and really didn't need to have it broken again, not to mention the whole point of the fielding drill failed because now I'm even more afraid of the ball than I ever was before.

This season they've moved me out to left field and I can say I'm a much better outfielder than I am an infielder, except when I have to rush a line drive. I always sit back and let it bounce once. I know you're supposed to try and hustle in to take it on a fly, but what can I say, two broken noses is enough for me.

During our last game, I had a double and a single but struck out twice. I was trying to kill the ball and when you do that, you usually take your eye off the ball because you're looking to see the ball sail over the home run fence.

"Keep your eye on the ball!" your coaches scream at you all game long. They scream it when you're at bat and when you're in the field. Obviously, I have a problem with that.

After the game, we went to Carvel to get ice cream. You only get ice cream if you win, and this summer our team isn't very good—to be honest, we suck—so this was only our second visit to Carvel. You're not allowed to order anything but a small cone, either chocolate or vanilla soft serve, with or without rainbow or chocolate sprinkles. No sundaes. No banana splits. No milkshakes. No exceptions. We stand on line against the counter waiting for Norman, the Carvel guy, and his son, Little Norman, to make our cones. I don't know if that's Little Norman's real name but that's what we call him. We have this joke we always tell when we're watching Norman and his son make our cones.

"How do the Normans take a shit?" We then squat down and move our ass around in a circle doing the same motion as the ice cream coming out of the machine. Old Norman turns around and gives us the stink eye because he knows we're joking about him but he doesn't know why, but Little Norman knows what we're saying and gives us the finger.

My mom usually comes to all my games because she's a big baseball fan. She grew up in the South Bronx just a few blocks from Yankee Stadium and if you live that close to the Bronx Bombers, you're going to be a big baseball fan. Her two older brothers Mike and Mark were Yankee fans too and the three of them would go to games all the time. She says that when she was little, the tickets were so cheap, kids went to the games by themselves all the time, which is pretty cool. But even cooler than that was how you got to your seats. You would enter the stadium from behind the home run wall and walk through the outfield, on the actual grass, to get to your aisle and walk up from there to your seat. I can't believe they don't do that anymore. I would love to actually step on the center field grass where Joe D. and Mickey Mantle and now Mickey Rivers chase down fly balls. Now you have to enter the stadium the regular way through the gates and up to your seats and you never get to go on the field unless they win the pennant or the World Series.

That's what happened two summers ago when the Yankees beat the Royals for the American League. All the fans rushed out onto the field to celebrate with the players. Louie was at that game and grabbed a chunk of grass from behind second base to take home with him. Louie loves Willie Randolph, the Yankees' second basemen, so that's why Louie fought through the crowd to get some grass from Willie's spot. He's now got this special section in his backyard where his dad replanted the grass and put a little fence around it so it won't get confused with the regular lawn. We'll look at it sometimes and we're amazed that Willie actually stood on that patch of grass. I asked my mom if she ever did the same thing when she was crossing the outfield to get to her seats and she says of course she didn't because they didn't have a backyard.

"And why would I need a chunk of grass when I could go to the stadium any day I wanted?"

She even went to Babe Ruth's wake when he died because they had the open casket at the stadium. She and her brothers and all the kids from the neighborhood waited on line all day with all the other Yankee fans to pay their respects. They didn't let you stop and kneel and say a prayer like I did at Pop's wake, but she says you could walk by and do the sign of the cross and say a quick little prayer.

My mom graduated high school in 1955 so when she was a kid, she got to see all the greats play, Mickey Mantle, Whitey Ford, Yogi Berra, Elston Howard, and of course her favorite, Joe DiMaggio. She lived on 161st Street off Sherman Avenue and Joe D. had an aunt who lived down the block from her apartment and the Yankee Clipper himself would go there sometimes for Sunday dinner. All the kids would be out on the sidewalk waiting for Joe to finish eating his Sunday supper so they could get his autograph. My mom said he would sign everything the kids had, and she and her brothers had a dozen baseballs signed by Jolting Joe, but she has no idea what happened to them. Can you imagine that? She said it wasn't a big deal to get an autograph back then because the Yanks were always around and would always stop and talk to the kids. She and her friends would also wait outside the Concourse Plaza Hotel, which was also just down the street from her apartment, because a lot of the Yanks and some of the players from the other teams would stay there during the season and they'd sign your stuff when they all walked over to the stadium for a game. I've asked her a hundred times to look for those old autographs but she says she doesn't know what happened to them.

"Who knows," she says, "They're just gone. Disappeared like everything else."

When I got home from Carvel and I tell her we finally won a game, she's upset that she missed it. She apologizes and takes my hand and she looks like she might even cry again. Oh boy, here we go again.

"I promise I'll be at the next game, but I just couldn't get out of work for this one."

She works at JFK. That's the airport near our house. She's not a stewardess or anything like that. She works for the FAA, in an office. I don't know what the FAA is or what she does there but she seems to love it because anytime she tells us a story about work and the people she works with, she always starts laughing in the middle of the story because she thinks they're so funny and she can never finish the story because she's cracking up so hard that it makes her cry, only these are happy tears.

But now she's got the gloomy look in her eyes and I'm worried the sad tears, not the laughing tears, might come again and I try to tell her it's not a big deal.

"You can come to the next game. It's on a Saturday."

"That's not the point. How many more games do you even have left? And how many more games will you even want your mother to come to?" she asks me.

I don't know why she thinks I won't have that many more

games because I still love baseball. Unless she thinks I'm not good enough to play in high school but that's still years away. I guess I can see her point about me not wanting her to come and watch my games when I'm older because that's what happened with Tommy when he got to high school, and she used to love to watch Tommy play because wasn't he as graceful as Joe D. himself when he was tracking down a fly ball or running around the bases.

I could tell the whole conversation is upsetting her so I changed the subject and asked her about her day, and she tells a funny story about her friend from work, Bunny from Bensonhurst, and again she laughs so hard she can't finish the story without asking for tissues for her happy tears.

15

If my dad is off from work during the week, Tommy always says the same thing: "Oh fuck, there goes my fun for the day." Because that means my dad will be home all afternoon and when you're a teenager you hate having your parents around, especially in the summer, because if you're just hanging out looking bored they're gonna tell you to get up off of your ass and do something, and if you can't find something to do I'll find something for you and you can start by cleaning out the garage.

Tommy used to love my dad's days off when he was little because instead of giving him chores to do like he does now, he would make them father and son days. This is when we'd go fishing, or take the dog for a walk at Bay Park, or go to the batting cage, or go visit our great-grandmother in Rockaway Beach, which usually meant we'd spend a few hours either at the Playland Amusement Park or go down under the Cross Bay Bridge to go crabbing. Tommy used to like all that stuff, because what kid wouldn't, but like my dad said a hundred times before, he's a teenager now and teenagers hate everything.

When my dad is home from work it also means family dinner in the dining room. I used to love family dinners because when we were younger everybody used to get along and tell funny stories and laugh a lot. Even my mom would be laughing and smiling the whole time and she would tell wild stories about her childhood in the Bronx with her two brothers: Mike, the sweet, good-looking one, who she adores, and Mark, the tough crazy one, who loved to fight and would protect her if any jerks were hitting on her in the bars. But now, the family dinners are less fun because Tommy's always moody and gloomy and doesn't say much other than short one-word answers. Like when my dad asks him, "What did you do with yourself today?"

"Nothing," Tommy says.

"Nothing? You did nothing all day? You had to do something. Tell me one thing you did."

"I ate lunch."

"OK, that's a start. With whom did you eat lunch?"

"Nobody you'd know."

"Try me."

"Joe Blow."

"And what did you eat with Mr. Blow?"

"I don't know. Food."

It can go on like this for the whole meal. So now our family dinners are just tense and usually end with someone yelling at someone—my dad yelling at Tommy or Tommy yelling at my mom or my mom yelling at my dad. I try to just keep my head down and finish my dinner because if you don't finish your dinner, you're gonna start getting yelled at too. Family dinners were so much better before all the yelling started. I'm sure this is why one night last month my dad went out to the bar to watch the Yankee game and my mom went to the movies by herself and I was given two bucks and sent up to Pizza Amore—"the pizza you love to eat"—to get a couple of slices.

As I sat there in the corner booth eating my slices, one regular and one Sicilian, I keep thinking about what my mom said on that St. Patrick's Day. "This isn't the life a young girl dreams of." I don't know why she would think that because I like our life, or at least, I used to like it before I ended up eating alone in the corner booth at Pizza Amore on a day when my dad was home from work, and we should all be eating together as a family.

Even before Pop died, it's been bad days like that all summer, but instead of just fighting, now my parents seem to hate each other. It got really ugly when my dad's car, a 1973 Ford Pinto, wouldn't start again. My dad was supposed to go work a midnight tour and because his partner Carmine had already left his house and couldn't pick him up, he was going to have to take the train into the city if he couldn't get the car going. I went out to the street to help because Tommy wasn't home even though he was grounded after coming home drunk the other night, but they have no control over him, so he just does what he wants.

My dad tells me to hold the flashlight as he works on the engine. He was doing something with the carburetor and was yelling at me to keep the light shining on where he was working but my arm kept getting tired and the light would move and my dad couldn't see what he was doing and that pissed him off. Finally, he said, "Fuck it, I'll take the goddamn Long Island Rail Road."

When he went into the house to grab his stuff my mom told him he should just call in sick. I don't know why that ticked him off even more, but it did, and that led to them yelling at one another. Whenever they yell like that, I run out to the backyard so I don't have to hear the mean things they say to one another so I can't really tell you what they were fighting about but after my dad left and slammed the door and walked up to the train station, my mom started crying. I didn't know what to do to make her feel better because these weren't the regular sad tears. These were bigger louder sobbing tears. If our old dog Kelly was still alive, she would have jumped up on the couch and started licking my mom's tears and that would have made my mom laugh and smile. I wish there was something I could do to make her laugh and smile but I can't and it's too weird to see her cry like this, so I just snuck down to the basement and played side one of *Live Rust* over and over. Talk about putting you in a mood. When you go from "Sugar Mountain" into "I Am a Child" to "Comes a Time" and then "After the Gold Rush," it's gonna bring you down. Finally, my mother came down and asks, "Why do you keep listening to the same sad songs over and over? Are you trying to torture yourself?" I shrug. I don't really know why I'm listening to sad songs over and over when I'm already sad enough. But I don't really know why I do anything.

That was the second really big screaming match they've had recently. Near the end of the school year, my dad came home from work one day and my mom was throwing all of his clothes out their bedroom window onto the front stoop. I'm not sure what that fight was about either because once the yelling started, I got on my bike and took off to Louie's house.

Me and Louie watched from his front stoop as my dad picked up his clothes off our front lawn and went inside. Louie didn't ask me what was going on and I didn't tell him. We just watched. I guess that's why we're such good friends. Sometimes you don't need to talk about stuff to know what's going on.

16

In the car going to Mass one day, my mom wants to know if I started reading any of the books she got me. I lie. I tell her I started *The Old Man and the Sea* because that's the only title I can remember. I ask her about her fight with dad and she lies and says it was nothing. So, I guess we're even. Two liars on their way to church.

A few weeks earlier, Tommy told me he thought my mom and dad might get a divorce. Of course, I blamed it on him for being such a jerk to both of them lately, but I didn't say that out loud because he would have kicked my ass. I don't know any divorced people even though most of my friends' parents seem to be fighting all the time. But we're all Catholic and Catholics don't get divorced and that's why my mom and dad won't split up either. I hope.

It's just me and my mom going to Mass this morning because my dad is working and won't be home until after dinner and Tommy's sleeping one off, not that he goes to church anymore, either with or without us. We park behind the church near the stone grotto eggshell with the giant statue of the Virgin Mary which is where you take your picture after your First Holy

Communion and your Confirmation, which I won't have to deal with until next year but I'm already dreading it because it's a ton of extra schoolwork and studying and it's all about God and Jesus and I hate to admit it, but that stuff is really boring and just makes you feel lousy about yourself because you can't possibly live up to the standards of all the saints.

The parking lot at the church also serves as the playground for my school but the Virgin Mother's eggshell is off limits. If you're playing kickball during recess and someone like T-Mac kicks the ball over everyone's head and it lands all the way next to the Blessed Mother, you better not think of getting it yourself because if you do, you're going to the Bull's office. But if you're in a tight game and it's almost the end of the lunch break and your team needs another at bat, you might risk it and make a mad dash to grab the ball, saying a quick prayer as you pass the Blessed Mother's statue that one of the lunch ladies doesn't see you.

But on a Sunday, you can go right up to the statue and take as much time as you want. You can even touch her feet if you want to—somebody once put nail polish on her toes—but there's no thrill in approaching the Mother of God if there isn't the threat of being sent to the Bull's, so me and my mom just walk past her with a quick genuflection on our way into Mass.

There is a giant old tree next to the side steps of the church. I have no idea what kind of tree it is. I just know it's not a maple, but like a maple, it has giant roots. My mom asks me if I remember the rat who lived under the tree and how we used to see him running along the roots and then disappear down into a hole in the wall of the church and how she turned that into my favorite bedtime story.

"'Matt Fat the Water Rat?' Of course I remember," I say. "Do you remember I brought him my Tonka dump truck so that he could have a set of wheels?" I ask her. Of course she remembers because she's like me—she remembers everything.

I gave Matt Fat the Water Rat my toy truck because I read this book in school—one that I actually liked—called *Runaway Ralph* about a mouse that could ride a toy motorcycle. So, because of this Runaway Ralph and his toy motorcycle, I wanted to leave something for Matt Fat the Water Rat, but since he was a pretty big fat rat and not a cute little mouse, I knew my matchbox cars would be too small for him, so one day we left my old Tonka truck under the big tree for Matt instead.

When we told my dad about the rat and the Tonka truck, he told the Monsignor, who asked my dad if the Father's Club would help get rid of the rat. The Father's Club is a group of dads who help out doing jobs around the school and church, like painting classrooms, fixing broken desks and tables, and I guess, thanks to my dad, killing rats. My dad actually started the Father's Club a few years ago because our school had a Mother's Club that did all sorts of charity events for the school like bake sales and white elephant sales where people sold their old junk so they could use the money to help the school and my dad thought the fathers should help out as well. So now, anytime there's a job that the Monsignor needs done, he calls my dad, including "taking out" Matt Fat the Water Rat.

When the deed was done, I was so upset I didn't talk to my dad for almost two weeks. Looking back on it, it woulda been so easy for him to have killed Matt Fat and hide it from me and have my mom tell me a bedtime story about how Matt Fat took the Tonka truck on a cross-country journey to be reunited with his brothers or some bullshit like that and I would have believed it because I was a little kid who still believed that rats could drive toy trucks. But no, that's not what happened. What happened was my dad took me with him to run some errands the next day.

When you're little, you like running errands with your dad, because if you're going up to the stores, you're going to walk by Carvel and nine times out of ten, your dad is going to ask if you want some ice cream, so that's why I always agreed to go with him to run some errands. But on this day, our first and only stop was to Henry's Hardware which also happens to be next door to Buzzy's Deli, so I thought we would at least go get some Ring Dings or some Yodels or a Hostess Coffee Cake if he said no to the ice cream but that didn't happen. I guess he was too focused on the job at hand.

Henry and Buzzy were two old German guys from the early days of the neighborhood when the Lutheran church would be packed to the gills and "those were the days, weren't they Buzzy?" Before "the flood gates from Brooklyn and Queens opened, and the wave of Irish and Italians and their big families showed up." My dad loves these two old timers because my dad loves old guys who tell old stories about the olden days even if they always mention how all the Catholic families like ours who came from the city ruined the place.

"Why they got ten kids if they got no farm? It doesn't make no sense. If you had a farm, you'd need those hands to work it. Otherwise, I don't understand why you'd want the ten and eleven kids in one house," Henry says.

Anytime we go into Buzzy's, he starts going into his stories about when he stormed the beach at Normandy on D-Day.

My dad will be in the middle of ordering a roast beef sandwich and Buzzy will decide that's a good time to show you his war wounds.

"I had just jumped off the Higgins boat, up to my waist in the water when this Nazi machine gun ripped my guts apart."

Buzzy pulls up his shirt and shows us his stomach which has the nastiest scars you've ever seen. He points to where the five bullets entered his belly and the big scar that the medics left when they cut him open and pulled out four of the bullets.

"They left one in for good luck," Buzzy laughs.

"Hey Buzz," my dad says, "maybe you show us the scars when we're in here buying a six pack but not after I just ordered a roast beef sandwich." Buzzy laughs again, even though the two of them have had this same conversation a hundred times before. My dad says Buzzy always tells that story to remind people that not all Germans were Nazis.

The other old German guy, Henry, is even older than Buzzy and like Buzzy, he tells the same stories every time we go into his hardware store.

"Have I ever told you about how the Green Acres Mall used to be the Curtiss Airfield and how Charles Lindbergh and Amelia Earhart used to fly out of there?"

"I don't think so," my dad says, and I look at my dad like he's lost his mind because we've heard this story a million times.

"When I was a kid, we used to sit at the end of the runway in the high grass and watch as the planes took off and landed. We'd lie on our backs and those planes were so close to us we could wave at the pilots, and they'd wave back. Even Charlie Lindbergh. It was incredible. And then they turn it into a god-damn shopping mall? Dummkopfs."

I love the word "dummkopf" because it sounds exactly like what it means. Buzzy calls everyone a dummkopf who comes up to his counter and hasn't already decided what they want to order.

"What the hell have you been thinking about for the last ten minutes, you dummkopf? You think I got all day for you to make up your mind. Next!"

If Buzzy called you a dummkopf and you didn't know what it meant, you would still know he was calling you an idiot because that's what it sounds like. It's like stooge. If you're called a stooge, you know that's not a good thing even if you never heard the word before. Schmuck, schlemiel, and schmegegge are all good ones too, but skeeve is probably my favorite. It means dirtbag, only worse. If you heard someone called a skeeve, you would know it means they're probably not so clean and neat. Right? Even the way it feels in your mouth when you say it—skeeve—tells you what it is. We got a family around the block we call the Skeevy O'Leavys and the name really fits because they have eight kids and each one is dirtier than the next. I don't need to tell you what the two old Lutherans thought of them when they moved into the neighborhood.

My dad then tells Henry a story he's told him a million times before, but Henry doesn't seem to remember either. This must be a thing old guys do, tell each other the same stories over and over again. I could understand if you tell your favorite story to a guy you just met but these guys seem to do it every single time they see one another.

"When I was a kid," my dad says, "We did the same thing, only at LaGuardia, when that was still a sleepy little airport. I went to school with a kid who moved to Astoria and in the summer we'd ride our bikes from his house to go fishing in the streams that used to run through the marsh over there and on our way home we'd hide in the bushes at the end of the runway and you'd lie on your back and watch these massive planes take off and land right over you. And Henry, let me ask you, as a little kid, was there anything more exciting than that?"

Henry doesn't answer him. He just nods with a smile on his face. And my dad nods with a smile on his face too. Then they both stand silently, just nodding and staring off into space, smiling. I guess that's why old guys like to tell these old childhood stories over and over again—it makes them smile.

Anyway, my dad tells Henry about Matt Fat the Water Rat and how the Monsignor wants the rat "taken care of." Henry nods, then goes behind the counter and comes back with five giant mousetraps.

"These will take care of your rat, no problem," he says. "But forget about using a piece of cheese like in the cartoons. What you do is you put some peanut butter in there. The rat loves the peanut butter. The mouse loves the cheese. But you also got to make sure you put down a lot of newspaper. Newspaper all over the floor and even try to tape some to the walls. Here, I'll give you some masking tape for that too. You need all this newspaper because when the rat goes to eat the peanut butter, this trap comes down so hard it will cut him in half so be careful of yourself when you set it up. You're not careful and you could lose a finger. The newspaper is for the mess so don't chintz on the newspaper because you don't want to have to scrub all that rat blood and guts off your Monsignor's walls."

On the way home, the rat traps are sitting in the passenger seat next to my dad because I refused to sit up front with him and the traps that will cut Matt Fat in half and spray his blood all over the walls. Instead, I jumped into the back of our Volkswagen so I wouldn't have to look at my dad, the rat killer. We had a VW Bug back then, and behind the back seat was this little cozy nook that I could squeeze into. So that's where I tucked myself and cried the whole way home.

When we parked at the house, I refused to come out, so my dad left me there. He kept the windows open so I could breathe but it still got too hot, and I eventually had to get out and do my crying in the backyard.

Every Sunday after that I would look for Matt Fat the Water Rat when we walked along the side of the church to Mass, but I never saw him again. Thanks, Dad.

17

When we got home from Mass I was starving because you're not allowed to have breakfast until after you had your communion. But now that I've made my sacrifice and done my Eucharist fast, I'm not interested in breakfast, I want milk and cookies but when I go to look for my cookies, they've already been eaten and it's only Sunday, so I know my brother Tommy must have eaten them last night when he came home drunk and stoned. You see, my mom goes shopping on Saturdays because she works during the week and she buys me and my brother one box of cookies each and "your box needs to last the whole week and if you eat all your cookies on the first day because you lack any kind of self-control then that's just too bad about you." This is exactly why my mom started buying us each our own box because Tommy would always eat all of our cookies the minute she brought them home from the store. Now if Tommy eats his cookies in one day, there's still cookies for me. But it never works out that way because Tommy's a dick, and he still eats all my cookies, and if I ever told on him, he'd kick my ass. So, I have a bowl of cereal with my milk instead.

But that night after dinner my dad asks if he can have some

of my cookies for desert and I have to tell him that mom must have forgotten to buy me some this week because I couldn't find any when I looked today after Mass. Of course, I know she didn't forget, and we all know who ate them.

My mom says, "What are you talking about? I went to the store yesterday. I got you your Oreos and your brother his Chips Ahoy."

She still calls them by the brand names even though last year we started buying the no-brand versions of all our food, and not just cookies but everything. We got the no-brand milk to go with your no-brand cereal, no-brand peanut butter to go with your no-brand jelly, and even no-brand spaghetti to go with your no-brand red sauce. No-brands come in black and white boxes and are cheaper than the regular brands. I have to admit it's a little embarrassing when your friends come over and everything in your food cabinet and in your fridge is in black-and-white no-brand boxes because it looks like you're a beggar who can't afford the regular brands.

My dad says, "What do you care what they look like? They all taste the same. Don't they?"

"Yeah, I guess."

"Then who gives a shit what your friends think? What are they, aristocrats? Are any of them rolling in the dough? Living on Park Avenue? I didn't think so."

They may not be rolling in the dough, but I think they must have more money than us because we've never had a new car and most of my clothes are hand-me-downs from Tommy and now we've got the no-brand food but of course I keep my mouth shut about any of that.

Anyhow, my dad wants my no-brand Oreos but there are

none to be had, so he looks to my brother Tommy, who says, "Why you looking at me?"

And my dad says, "Because you're guilty. Now get your ass up to the deli and buy a new box of cookies for your brother. Pronto!"

Tommy gets up from the table to go to the store but shoots me a look that says, "I'm gonna kick your ass when I get home tonight." But Tommy doesn't get my cookies and Tommy doesn't kick my ass that night because Tommy doesn't come home for a few days. When he finally does come home, my parents don't even yell at him or ground him because they know it's hopeless.

"What are we gonna do?" my father says. "In six months, he'll be old enough to join the army. Let them figure him out."

Now that they have given up on Tommy, it gives him the green light to give me a couple of dead legs, put me in a head-lock, and call me a momma's boy when he finally does make it home. In the past he used to make me swear I wouldn't tell my mom and dad because that's what a pussy would do and like always, I would never rat. But now, he doesn't even bother with the warning, and I just get the beating.

18

I had a feeling Pop McSweeny was sick a few months ago when we drove our new car up to the Bronx to visit him and Gilligan. By the way, our "new" car isn't really a new car. Like I already told you, we don't buy new cars, we just buy old used clunkers and after my dad couldn't figure out why our last clunker, the Pinto, wouldn't start, he had it towed up to the Exxon station and Mugsy, our car mechanic, told my dad it was time for the junkyard.

"Ashes to ashes," my dad said because the fenders, the rear bumper, the driver's side door, and most of the engine we'd also bought at the junkyard.

When your dad brings home a new used car every couple of years, each one worse than the next, it can be a little embarrassing. Maybe even more embarrassing than the no-brand food. But this car is even worse and not just because it's a lousy car but because my dad bought this new piece of junk off one of the families we go to school with. And what makes it even more humiliating is this family is one of the dirtbag families whose kids never seem to wash and have greasy hair with dandruff and their clothes are all wrinkly and stained and I'm sure they must never shower because they have the worst BO you ever smelled. There's a few families at our school like that. Even the parents seem unwashed. As my dad says, "Cleanliness isn't high on their list of priorities." That musta carried over to their car too. When I jumped into the back seat for the first time the floor was covered with old newspapers, empty soda cans, candy wrappers, a few smelly old beach towels, and two cans of oil. Guess who got the job of cleaning it up?

The family that owned this jalopy of a Delta 88 have a son who is a few years older than me. His name is Phillip Phillips. I don't get why his parents would name him Phillip if their last name is Phillips. It's bad enough to have the same name as your first and last name, because that's just weird, but when your initials are P. P. you're gonna get ragged on every day of your life because everybody is gonna call you P. P. But it isn't P. P., it's Pee Pee and when kids say it, they pretend to be holding their peckers and taking a piss. He's also called Piss Pot and Pin Prick and Pig Pen, like the character in Charlie Brown who's so dirty he walks around surrounded by a cloud of dirt. And that's this kid too, he's that dirty.

Now if I'm a kid whose parents don't make me shower and clean my ears and wash my hair and scrape the shit out from under my fingernails, I wouldn't make things worse by also being the kid who still picks his nose and eats it, but that's what Piss Pot does, and he doesn't try to hide it either. He'll sit there at a lunch table in the middle of the cafeteria clawing up his nose like he's digging for gold and pulling out a giant wet one that hangs off his dirty finger. The runny snot is so long and gooey that, in order to eat it, he has to stick his tongue out and tilt his head to the side to get under the booger. He doesn't seem to care that every kid in the school is watching him because the whole cafeteria will start chanting "Pee Pee Pig Pen Piss Pot" until the Bull looks up from her desk at the front of the lunchroom with her mean eyes and her red face and everyone goes quiet. But then he still eats the booger.

I ask my dad, "Why did we have to buy their car?"

He said, "Because it was for sale and the price was right. Why? Do you have a problem with it?"

"No," I say. He's in a bad mood so I decide not to mention all the dried boogers I found on the bottom of the back seat when I had to clean up all the old newspapers, empty soda cans, candy wrappers, smelly beach towels, and oil cans because I knew if I mentioned the boogers I'd have to clean them and I am not touching no stinking dried-out snot rockets.

When Tommy sees the new car, he calls it the "Shit Mobile" because it's brown with an all-brown interior and "it's a total piece of shit." I guess I should be used to having a crappy old car like the Shit Mobile because we've always had crappy old cars except in 1972 when we got a brand-new Chevy Impala. I was too young to really remember that car, but I've seen it in family pictures. It got stolen when my dad took it into work one day. Can you believe someone would actually steal a policeman's car right off the street when it's parked down the block from the precinct?

"But that's New York, kid. Land of the free, home of the brazen," he says. "And that's why we don't buy new cars anymore."

On the drive to the Bronx, it had started raining, which made me feel better because it meant I wouldn't be missing out on anything fun with my friends. Me and Tommy sit in the back seat of the Shit Mobile and for no reason at all, Tommy starts punching me in the thigh and giving me dead legs. My father threatens to pull the car over to smack the crap out of him but my mom just wants peace and quiet, so she tells me to jump in the front seat and sit between her and my dad. Tommy loves this because now he can lie down and have the whole back seat to himself. Within minutes, he's snoring, sleeping off another hangover.

As we drive, I point out all the cars on the side of the road that have been stripped. Anytime your car dies and you have to leave it on the side of the highway to get gas or find a pay phone to call a tow truck, you're pretty much guaranteed that by the time you get back, something will be stripped from it. If you're only gone for a little while, it's usually just the hub caps. If you're gone for a long time, they'll take the tires too. But if you have to leave it overnight, everything will be gone, doors, fenders, bumpers, seats, even the steering wheel.

My mom is terrified this new piece of crap we're driving will break down and we'll have to pull over on the Grand Central Parkway and sit in the car and wait for my dad to return with the tow truck. That happened once last winter on the Cross Bronx. Our old Pinto's gas gauge was broken so anytime my dad put gas in the car, he'd write down on an index card he kept clipped to the visor how many gallons he put in and what the mileage was. This way he could keep track of when he needed to fill it up. So that day last December, when the old Pinto started sputtering and then just died right in the middle of the highway, my dad knew something was fishy. It was embarrassing enough we caused a traffic jam, but it got even worse when me and Tommy had to help my dad push the car to the side of the road and all the crazy New York drivers were honking and screaming and yelling at us and calling us schmucks and assholes and cocksuckers. My dad isn't the kind of guy to let people talk to his kids like that, so he was cursing back at them, giving them the finger, telling guys to pull over and say that to his face while my mom sat behind the steering wheel yelling at us to just keep pushing for Christ's sake. When we finally got the car on the shoulder my dad grabbed Tommy.

"I'll give you one chance to tell me the truth. Did you and your asshole friends take the car out this week?"

Tommy nodded. I knew he'd tell the truth because our dad is a cop, and they get trained to tell when someone is lying to them.

"So, it's bad enough that you stole my car and took it without permission when you don't even have a driver's license, but you're also too stupid to cover your tracks and fill the tank with gas?"

Tommy shrugs.

"That's all you have to say for yourself?"

Tommy says, "I didn't think I used that much gas."

That pisses my father off because Tommy says it like he could give a shit.

"So, because of your stupidity and your arrogance and your thoughtlessness I have to go try and find a gas station and leave you and your little brother and your mother by the side of the road. But you know what? I'm not gonna do that, you're gonna do that."

My mom stepped in. "You are not going to let him walk down this highway alone, let alone send him up into the South Bronx to find a gas station."

"What's the alternative option? I go and leave all of you by the side of the road? Or we all walk to find a gas station and leave the car here for the vultures? He's seventeen. He can handle it. And it's his fault we're in this mess."

Dad gave Tommy a gas can and the lug wrench from the trunk, which on a Ford Pinto is actually in the front of the car because the engine is in the back. This was a problem for Pinto drivers and their passengers because if you got rear-ended in a Pinto, the car could explode, which is why the Pinto was sometimes called the "Barbecue That Seats Four." Anyway, my dad told Tommy to walk up the Cross Bronx to the next exit and find a gas station.

"The can is for the gas. The wrench is for anybody who might try to jump you."

Luckily, no one tried to jump him, and he was back with some gas in an hour.

To get to the Bronx from our house we usually take the Throgs Neck Bridge but today we take the Cross Island to the Grand Central to the Triborough and then cut through Manhattan and over the Willis Avenue Bridge. When we take this route we drive past the big park in Flushing Meadows near Shea Stadium, where they held the 1964 World's Fair. Every time we pass by this spot, my dad will tease my mom about the Greek guy she dated before she met my dad.

"Here we go boys. Get ready to hear all about Benny Baklava and what a grand time your mother had at the World's Fair."

Mom just laughs. "His name was not Baklava and you know it. And he was a very nice young man."

I guess Benny the Greek was some kind of champion

swimmer or something and he performed in the water shows they did during the World's Fair. Because my mom would go watch Benny the Greek anytime he performed, she spent a lot of time at the World's Fair and knows everything about the place. Her favorite attraction to point out is the ruins of the Aqua Theater because that's where Benny did his thing. It's falling apart now and it's another thing that breaks my mom's heart.

"Boys, you should have seen what it was like in '64. It was like walking into the future," she said. "It gave you a feeling of such promise. And now look at it. In ruins. Rusted and rotting."

She goes on to tell us all about the Unisphere, which is that huge globe of the world you can still see from the highway. She points out the New York Pavilion with the Tent of Tomorrow and its three observation towers, which are now covered in fifteen years' worth of pigeon shit. I ask her about the two old rocket ships that are still there, and she says they're all that's left of the Space Park. I love to see the rocket ships and I've got my face pressed up to the window to get a better look but it's raining harder now and it's tough to see anything.

I got to admit, it's always a little depressing to see this place my mom loves so much is now ruined, rotting and rusting, but on a rainy day like this, it's even more gloomy. As we drive away from the old World's Fair site my mom gets quiet and I see the sadness in her eyes is back. And I can feel I've got the sadness in my eyes as well. Maybe the sadness is contagious or maybe it's a family trait, like the freckles on my nose I got from my mom that she says she got from her mom even though she doesn't remember any freckles on her mom because her mom died when she was young and she barely remembers anything about her and there is just the one picture of her on the deck of the boat coming over from Ireland and it's old and grainy and in black and white so you can't tell if she has freckles or not but Pop McSweeney said oh she was a beauty with a face full of freckles and that's where you get them from young man, so you do.

The sadness continued when we got to Pop and Gilligan's because Pop was getting old and must have already been sick because he barely got up from his chair. It made me feel weird to see him so weak with the life all but out of him and I remember feeling guilty that I didn't want to be there because when I was little, I used to love coming over to his apartment. Maybe it was because I was getting older and when you get older, hanging out with grandparents just starts to get boring. But I think it was mostly because Pop couldn't do the stuff he used to do that made it fun to be with him.

Pop used to take me and Tommy up to their roof because you can see Yankee Stadium from there and if a game is going on you could hear the crowd and the announcers and the organ like you were right there in the stands even if you couldn't see the field. Pop didn't like baseball because he was a Paddy-off-the-boat, but he knew we did, so he always made sure we came to visit on game days. But today's game was rained out, so we didn't go up to the roof.

If it wasn't baseball season, he would invite us out onto the fire escape when he went out there to smoke his pipe. After he married Gilligan, he started having to smoke his pipe outside because she didn't like the smell of tobacco and wouldn't let him smoke in the apartment. I thought that was crazy because I loved the smell and now anytime I get a whiff of someone smoking a pipe I think of Pop.

"Lads, step out here to my office and let us discuss the state of the world, shall we now?" he would tell us as he climbed out his window.

Tommy and I would join him out there and sit on old wooden milk crates as he stood against the railing and looked out down the street to the Grand Concourse. As he lit his pipe and smoked it, you had no choice but to stare at his hands. Hands like Thurman Munson's catcher's mitt, as my dad would say, because they were huge and swollen and his fingers were as thick as Italian sausages and crooked from getting broken all the time at work.

"You can't spend a life smashing rock without smashing a few of your fingers in the process. So you can't," Pop would say.

Pop was a sandhog, which is kinda like a miner, only instead of digging for coal or diamonds, they build tunnels, like the Lincoln Tunnel, which is the job Pop is most proud of. Anytime we go to New Jersey to visit my mom's brothers, Mike and Mark, we always take the Lincoln.

"That's my father's handiwork all around us," my mom says as we drive through the tunnel from Manhattan. When we drive through the Lincoln there's no sadness in her eyes, only pride.

When we'd get to my Uncle Mike's house, Pop would be there sitting in the kitchen, smoking his pipe, because in Mike's house a man can enjoy his pipe and not be chased out onto the fire escape to face the elements, so he can.

"You take the Lincoln?" Pop would ask when we arrived.

"We did."

"And you know who gave years of his life to that tunnel so you and yours wouldn't have to take a ferry across the Hudson, don't you?"

"We do."

"We did a fine job too, that tunnel is a piece of history that will live on long after we're all gone, even if my years digging that hole will end up being the death of me."

You see, when they build tunnels, they dig down really deep into the ground and then put dynamite sticks into the bedrock and blow it up. The sandhogs then go down into the hole and pick up all these huge chunks of broken stone and lug them into the mining carts to be carried out.

"But the tunnel is thick with tiny bits of rock and stone dust floating about and as you breathe, you can feel the air has to fight its way down your throat, so it does."

It sounds like the worst job you could ever have, especially when you see the state of Pop's hands and I always wondered why didn't he just become a bread baker when he got here to America because that's what he did in Ireland and I know he was happy baking bread because he's got a picture hanging in his hallway of when he's young and smiling and standing proudly in front of the McSweeney's Bakery wagon with his horse, Terrence Joseph—who, let it be known, was the finest horse in all of County Westmeath, so he was, and I still miss him till this day, so I do.

"But that was hard work too, waking up before the sun to stand in front of a hot oven all day but not nearly as hard as heading down into the hole to dig out the rock and suck in the dust," he'd say. "But there was no call for an Irish baker in the Bronx when the place was crawling with Italians."

My absolute favorite visits to Pops used to be on Saturdays

because after dinner all his old Irish friends would show up for a session. It was usually the same three guys but sometimes there could be nine or ten of them. There was Brady, the guy who played the fiddle at the wake, and another guy who played a guitar and another guy named Frankie who played the accordion. Pop didn't play any instruments, but he could sing. As the band would play, Pop would pick us up to sit us down on the kitchen counter and say, "Pay attention lads, these are the songs that tell our story." He and the men would then play and sing and dance for hours. Even my mom and dad would join in. My dad didn't know the words to any of the old Irish songs but of course my mom knew them all from the times she sat on the bars in all the pubs along Third Avenue waiting for Pop to finish his pint and finish his song before sending her home on the El with what was left of his paycheck.

One day out on the fire escape, Pop let me and Tommy take a drag on his pipe. Tommy said he liked it and didn't cough at all. I guess I did it wrong because I couldn't stop coughing for ten minutes and Gilligan heard me and knew what Pop did and she yelled at him.

"Isn't that just grand, letting the boys smoke from your pipe. And the next thing you know, you'll be taking them down to the pub for a pint, so you will."

Pop winks and we laugh as Gilligan walks off in a huff. "Next year lads, we'll go for that pint," he says.

But next year is here and we won't go for that pint because Pop is gone.

On the drive home I ask if we can stop at the Fulton Fish Market, but my parents say it's been a long day and they're tired and just want to get home.

"Besides, at this hour we'll just take the Throgs Neck and be home in no time," she says.

The Fulton Fish Market, if you don't know, is this place in Manhattan where all the fish for New York City gets delivered before it then goes out to all the seafood shops and restaurants. My dad took us there a few years ago on our drive home from Uncle Mike's house. It was really late, maybe three or four in the morning, and we had taken the Lincoln Tunnel into Manhattan to take the Brooklyn-Battery Tunnel into Brooklyn to take the Belt Parkway out to Long Island.

"Let's take the boys to see the fish market," my dad said that night. "They should see it when it's really up and running."

"At this hour? No. Let's just get home already," my mom said.

"It's two minutes out of our way. And there's nobody on the road anyhow."

"But knowing you, you'll get to talking to somebody and we'll be there till the sun is up."

I held my breath because I had seen this before. This was another one of those moments where my parents could launch into a big fight depending on what my dad would say next.

"Come on, I think the boys will enjoy it. Especially Tommy." Tommy used to love fishing and this was years ago when he was still a nice kid and he started begging my mom to please let us go and like I told you, Tommy used to be her favorite, so of course, she had to say yes, but you could tell she was still pissed about it.

The Fulton Fish Market is the craziest place you've ever seen. There were tons of trucks blocking all the streets and gangs of all these working guys in aprons and rubber boots pushing carts back and forth across the street from the docks to the warehouses and all the trucks and all the carts are packed with all kinds of fish. They had tuna, salmon, sword, sea bass, striped bass, sea scallops, bay scallops, clams, mussels, lobster, and my mother's favorite, oysters.

"Your mother thinks she's some kind of aristocrat with her taste for the oysters," my dad said.

Of course my dad did know one of the main guys there, who he called the Professor, and of course the Professor was happy to see my dad, because my dad had helped him out when the Professor's son got jammed up for stealing a car so the Professor had a few dozen oysters as a gift for my mom so she wouldn't be so mad when we were still at the fish market as the sun was coming up just like she said we would be. The Professor also explained to us that oysters used to be so cheap you could even buy them on the street corner from a guy with a cart like you can buy a frankfurter from the hot dog stand today.

"That's how Pearl Street got its name. But not from the pearl of the oyster but because so many people ate oysters and then dumped their shells on the street, the whole block looked as shiny as a pearl."

"You see that," my dad said, "That's why he's called the Professor. Because he knows more about the fish market than anybody else in New York."

I loved every second of it—the fishmongers yelling at the truck drivers and the truck drivers screaming at each other, the boats at the dock unloading the fish, and the fish being put on ice in the old wooden stalls. It was all so busy and loud and exciting—except for the smell.

"If you got a sensitive nose, kid, then Fulton Street ain't for you," said the Professor.

When the sun came up and we got back in the car to drive home, my mom smiled at my dad and said, "The boys enjoyed that. I'm glad we stopped, despite the smell."

Since then, anytime I smell fish, I don't think of the any of the fishing trips I've taken with my dad, I think of the Fulton Fish Market and my mom's smile in the front seat. But tonight, we don't stop on Fulton Street, we just drive straight home and there are no smiles in the front seat.

19

It's a funny thing with smells. How they can take you back to a time and a place. The smell of fish, Pop McSweeney's pipe, and my mom's perfume all do that to me. I don't know what brand she wears but if some lady in a store is wearing that same perfume it always reminds me of this one day years ago when she dragged me into the city to go shopping with her at Macy's to buy my dad a Father's Day gift. I really didn't want to go because what kid wants to go shopping with their mother. And to make it even worse, we were schlepping into Manhattan which meant it was gonna be an all-day affair. I forget what we got him but it was probably a sweater or some gloves or a tie and I'm sure we could have found it at the Green Acres Mall near our house, but my mom loves the city and she'll use any excuse she can to jump onto the train to get back in there.

Usually, I hate these trips but what made that day special was after we left Macy's we went for a walk all the way up to Central Park which is over twenty blocks away. We took Fifth Avenue up because my mom says there's no finer street in all the world and she held my hand the whole time. I was younger then, so I was happy to hold her hand and even if I was older I still woulda been happy to hold her hand because it's not like anyone in the city was going to recognize me and rag on me for being a momma's boy. That was the day I realized my mom was pretty because as we walked, men in suits and guys standing on corners and even a cop directing traffic all turned and smiled at her as we walked by. And she smiled back and there was no sign of the sad eyes that day.

When we got close to the park, we stopped in front of a jewelry store to look in the window. There was a diamond necklace behind the glass, and she told me that one day you're going to be so successful you're going to buy your mother something like that. Instead of the necklace, we got a couple of dirty water dogs and sat on a bench in Central Park and looked at the ducks. As we sat there more men in suits walked by and smiled and said hello and my mom smiled back. Something felt weird about all this smiling, so I got up and threw some of my hot dog bun to the ducks.

"Wouldn't that be something? To live up there with a view of the park?" she said as she pointed to the big apartment buildings. "When I was in high school, me and my girlfriends would walk through here during our lunch period and pick out which Fifth Avenue penthouses we were going to live in when we got married."

I told her I wouldn't want to live in the city. I told her I liked our house and our backyard and our front stoop and our block and if we lived here, I'd miss all those things.

She said, "That's just because that's all you know. That's why I took you to the city today. There's a big world out there and you need to be aware of it. There's more to life than Marlboro Road."

She gets quiet again, so I turn around and pretend to look at the ducks. A few minutes later, she's up and takes my hand.

"Come on. It's getting late. We don't want to be in the park after dark." Thankfully she doesn't tell me about how safe the park used to be when she was a girl and how you could walk from Fifth Avenue all the way across to Central Park West without a worry in the world because that's what she says any-time anyone mentions Central Park.

When we get to Columbus Circle, we take the subway back to Penn Station. Sitting on the train, she can't help herself.

"It breaks your heart this city, doesn't it," she said. "One minute you're on Fifth Avenue looking at a gorgeous necklace in the window of Tiffany's like you're some kind of Audrey Hepburn, and the next you're on a graffiti-covered subway train stepping around some poor soul sleeping on a cardboard box."

What do you say to that? I can't tell her I think the graffiti looks cool and I'd rather sit on the train and watch all the dif-ferent people and listen in on their conversations than look at a necklace in the window of a store and have strange men wink and whistle at my mom.

Of course when we get to Penn Station she starts talking about the old Penn Station and how they tore it down when she was in her twenties and what a gorgeous building it was and how she and her girlfriends from work came down there during their lunch breaks to protest the demolition but it did no good and how they cried as the wrecking balls swung and nobody seemed to give any thought to the craftsmen who cut the stone and chiseled the marble because no one thinks of those things in the same way that no one thinks of her father when they drive through the Lincoln Tunnel but thank goodness for Jackie O., or they would have done the same thing to Grand Central Station.

When we got on the Long Island Rail Road, I was so tired from all our walking and even more tired from hearing about how things used to be and how terrible things are now that I just wanted to take a nap but she stopped me when I put my face down on the empty seat next to us because who knows who was sitting here before us so she folded her coat up as a pillow and I fell asleep with my head in her lap and with the smell of her perfume in my nose.

20

That night when I got home my dad told me he went into my room and read some of my pages—without permission.

"Can you blame me? I saw the state of the place and figured I'd do you a favor and hang up the wet towel and bathing suit you left on the floor and then I happen to see you had some of your work on the desk, so I took a peek. If you hung up your shit, I woulda never come in here. So, in a way, it's your own fault."

I thought he was gonna kill me because of all the cursing and finding out about smoking a cigarette on the cliffs in Montauk and taking a sip of beer under the table on St. Patrick's Day but instead, he asks, "How the hell do you remember all those friggin' details?"

I shrug because who the hell knows how you remember stuff.

"I'm impressed kid," he says. Then he adds, "Tomorrow, let's take a ride."

The next day we get in the Shit Mobile and drive to the public library where my father tells me to go find something to read. I'm not really in the mood to look for a book because it's a perfect sunny day and who wants to read in the summer anyhow and I've already got the stack of books my mom wants me to read, and I haven't even looked at any of those yet.

In the front of the library, by the big window that looks out onto the street, they have this little pond with goldfish and lily pads, so I sit there on the rock wall and just look at the goldfish and wish my dad had asked me to go fishing instead.

Finally, when he comes over, he asks, "You find anything?"

"No," I say.

"Hard to find something if you don't look," he says, and I can tell he's disappointed in me.

I shrug and say nothing because I'm pissed at him for reading my stuff without my OK.

"But don't worry yourself," he says. "I picked out a book for you." Oh, great.

He hands me this book that looks even more boring than *Long Day's Journey Into Night*.

"You see that title," he says. "*Remembrance of Things Past?* That's what your stories made me think of."

"Is it any good?" I ask him.

"Why don't you just read it and decide for yourself."

"Do you think I'll like it?" I ask him.

"I have no idea. But the librarian recommended it."

"So why should I read a book I might not like?" I know I'm being a dick, but I'm still pissed.

"Because not everything in life is for your amusement. Sometimes you got to do certain things that you don't want to do, to better yourself."

Parents don't understand that is the worst way to try and get a kid to do something you don't want to do. Who wants to better themselves? It's the same horseshit reason they give you for eating vegetables.

As we drive home, he makes me read the first line of the book.

"First lines are important. It's like the first bite of a hamburger or a slice of pizza, you're gonna know immediately whether or not you're in for a good lunch."

So, I read the line. "For a long time, I used to go to bed early."

"What do you think?" he asks.

"I don't know."

"Well, is it a good line or not? Does it make you want to read more?"

"Maybe?"

"Why?"

"I don't know. I guess I want to know why he doesn't go to bed early anymore?"

"OK, so then it's a good first line because it's asking you to read the next line. Right?" I shrug again.

Like all of my friends' parents, neither my mom or my dad went to college. They've each talked about wanting to go back and take classes, but they don't have the time or the money so instead, they bug me and Tommy about it all the time. Sometimes they say it in direct ways like, "I'm working so many hours chasing bad guys so that you can go to college." Other times they do it like my dad did today with library trips, giving us books, asking us to read, making us look up words in the dictionary or sometimes even making us watch classical music concerts on PBS. I'm telling you right now, if going to college means I have to listen to classical music, I'm not going.

When we get home, my dad sends me up to my room to read at least one chapter of one of the books.

"After that, you can go hang out on the block, and tomorrow, you can tell me who's more entertaining—the knuckleheads on the street corner or the words of a good book," he says.

I look at all the books in front of me, the one we just got from the library and the ones my mom bought me. I lined them up on my desk in order of thickness and decided to try *The Old Man and the Sea* because of all the books, it's the skinniest. I also know it's about fishing and I love fishing so hopefully it won't suck too bad.

21

We were going to spend that weekend with my great-grandma, Svenska, out in Rockaway Beach. Svenska isn't her real name, it's just what my dad calls her because she's from Sweden. Her real name is Octavia, but I've never heard anybody call her that. Me and Tommy call her Grandma Down the Beach because she spends her summers in a little bungalow just two blocks from the ocean.

I'm not sure how old she is. But she seems older than Mr. Ford so I'm guessing she's got to be close to one hundred but she can still cook and clean and tell funny stories. Usually really old people make you feel weird because they can be hard to look at. They might have weird marks and blotches on their faces and hands, or their skin is so loose it hangs off their bones or their hair is so thin you can see through to their scalps which isn't so bad for the old guys but it makes you feel bad for the old ladies because they try to doll up those last little strands into a hair style. Even though Grandma Down the Beach has almost no hair left and has the marks and the blotches and the thin skin, she doesn't give me the weird uncomfortable feelings. Maybe it's because she's always smiling and laughing. My dad says she smiles because she spends her summers at the beach.

"If you can look out and see the ocean every day, you too would have a smile plastered on your face," he says.

Because she's so old, she's lived through so many different decades, and she loves to tell you about all the stuff she's seen in her life.

"I was here before running water, before the car, before the plane, before the rockets to the moon, before the two World Wars and all that death. I was here before the radio and the record player and the movies and the TV, when the only thing you could do to keep yourself entertained was to read and think, and of course, tell stories," she says.

Svenska is another one who loves to tell the old stories. I can't really remember any of the stories she's told me about her growing up on a farm in Sweden or her boat ride over to Ellis Island, but I love her stories about her life in New York when she worked as a laundress for some rich New York City family.

"One of the few Catholic families on Fifth Avenue. They even had Cardinal Pacelli stay with us, who later became Pope Pius the Twelfth. And who do you think cleaned and steamed his robes during his stay?" she would ask us.

"What about his dirty drawers? You clean those too?" my dad asked.

"You are terrible, and you always have been," she said to my dad. "Is nothing sacred anymore?" She shook her head and asked me to grab the rosaries off her bedpost that were blessed by the very same Pope Pius the Twelfth whose robes she washed and pressed when he was still just a Cardinal. When I came back with the rosary beads, she makes me pray with her.

"We'll pray for your father and his inappropriate jokes," she said.

I pray along.

"I believe in God, the Father Almighty, the maker of heaven and earth," and so on and so on.

My mom always asks Svenska about the Fifth Avenue mansion because she loves those stories as well. Probably because that's where she always dreamed of living. I love them too because we don't know any rich people and I've never been in a mansion of any kind, so I hang on every word as Svenska describes the big dining room with ceilings so high you could play basketball in there, and the old library with the pool table and all the paintings on the walls of rich guys on horses hunting with their dogs, and the huge marble staircase in the front hallway that the servants weren't allowed to use—unless you were sweeping or mopping or polishing—because the staff had to take the back stairs off the kitchen, and how the servants lived on the top floor and had to share one bathroom and slept in these tiny little rooms that just had enough space for a sliver of a bed and a lamp but they had the best views of Central Park, even better than the master bedroom because they were on the top floor above the tree line.

"And I might still be there today if I hadn't met your great-grandfather and fallen in love with him the minute I laid eyes on him even though he was Irish and from the West Side and I knew those Irish boys from the West Side were nothing but trouble. But we like trouble, don't we?"

Svenska looked to my mom when she says that. My mom nodded and smiled but you could see she didn't feel the same way.

Svenska's husband was a guy named Eddie Fitzgerald and he was a stonecutter by day and a drummer in the speakeasy band by night. Speakeasies, if you don't know, were secret bars and restaurants during the 1920s when drinking was illegal. So, if you wanted to get your load on, that's where you had to go. When I think about all the booze that my family drinks now, my relatives from the olden times must have been in the speakeasies all the time.

"Can you imagine that? I'm a laundress cleaning the bedsheets for the future Pope Pius the Twelfth himself and Eddie Fitz is drumming in an underground gin joint surrounded by dancing girls and gangsters," Svenska says.

I'd smile and laugh like I know what the heck she was talking about, but I don't. I do that sometimes instead of saying I don't understand something or asking a question because, in my family, if you say you don't understand or you ask the wrong question you're gonna get ragged on and be accused of being dumber than a stump or not using the sense that God gave you or asked if you've got shit for brains. So sometimes it's best to just smile and laugh.

"But I loved my dear Edward from that first time I saw him until he choked out his last breath," Svenska says. "And even though he was surrounded by beautiful dancing girls every night, and let me tell you some of those girls—they were not the kinda ladies you'd want your husband around—he only had eyes for me."

Svenska loves talking about Eddie Fitz but I change the subject because I want to hear more about the mansion and less about the dancing girls.

"Can you tell me about the time you took my dad to the mansion?" I asked.

"I took your father to work with me a few times. Do you remember? I took you up to the roof where we hung and dried the laundry?" Svenska asked my dad.

"I do," said my dad.

"What else do you remember? Anything?"

"Not much. I was little."

"You don't remember the kitchen? How could you not remember the kitchen? Mr. O'Reardon, the cook, certainly remembered you. Charging in there, going straight for the sugar bowl, eating as many cookies as any boy he'd ever seen, drinking giant glasses of milk. You don't remember any of that?"

"I remember we couldn't go in through the front door. That we had to go through the side alley on Eighty-Third Street."

"That's what you remember? Always with the chip on your shoulder. 'How come we can't go through the front door?' he would complain. We were the servants, that's why," Svenska said.

"You asked what I remember. That's what I remember," my dad answered.

"You know what I remember, Svenska?" my mom said.

"Oh no, here she goes. Are we going to hear about the socks and underwear again?" my dad asked.

"Do you want to hear what Svenska did with me the first time I came to visit their apartment?" my mom asked me.

Of course, I said yes, even though I've heard this story a million times, but that's what old people do. Tell their stories over and over and who am I to get in the way.

"Svenska took me into your father's room to show me how she folded his underwear and socks. Told me he had very specific ideas about how he liked the undies folded and put away. Can you believe that? Like he was the one who lived on Fifth Avenue."

"If I couldn't go in the front door and use the main stairs, I'd at least have a socks and underwear drawer that looked like I did."

We all laughed, except Svenska. My parents love that story and when I think about it, it reminds me of when they used to laugh together all the time.

I promised myself I was going to make sure I ask my mom and dad to tell that story when we get to Svenska's bungalow because maybe it will remind them of when they used to smile and get along. My hope was just being down at the beach would put them in a better mood because my parents love Rockaway because that's where they met and of course everyone is in a better mood when they can look out and see the ocean.

Although, Rockaway is another place that can bring on my mom's sadness.

"Oh, you should have seen it back when it was called Irish Town, with all the Irish dance halls and bars on every corner and the boardwalk and beaches packed with people."

My parents have all these great old pictures from those days and it's funny to see pictures of your mom and dad when they're young and hanging out on the boardwalk arm in arm or at the beach with their friends wearing their bathing suits or dressed up at parties with beers in their hands and you can tell by the looks on their faces that they're drunk but they're happy. They have one picture where they're posing outside the Mermaid Bar, which is where they first met. It's a summer day and they're holding hands, and my mom is looking at the camera with a big smile on her face and my dad is looking at my mom like he can't believe his good luck. That's a picture they need to look at again to remind them of how happy they used to be.

Svenska has some of these old Rockaway pictures on the wall in her bungalow. Her favorite is a shot of my dad as a little kid on the boardwalk. He's sitting on the railing holding a fishing pole and behind him you can see row after row of bungalows, going from the beach all the way to the elevated Long Island Rail Road tracks. But all that is gone now, except the train tracks. Most of Irish Town and its bars and dance halls and bungalows were torn down in the '60s and '70s. Like the old Penn Station and the World's Fair in Queens and the theater in Times Square where my mom and dad saw Frank Sinatra on their first date, they've all been torn down.

Now when we drive from our house under the Long Island Rail Road tracks, we pass block after block of empty lots right on the beach and the only thing that remains from those days are the fire hydrants. But the good news is Svenska's bungalow on Beach 101st Street still stands and that's where we're going and that should make them happy.

22

My dad made me bring one of my new books, so I took *The Old Man and the Sea*. I tried reading it the other night but I just couldn't get into it so I was really hoping he wouldn't bug me about it once we got to Svenska's and maybe he'd forget that he made me bring a book, but it rained all day that Saturday, so we couldn't go to the beach, and Svenska didn't want to play gin rummy with me like she usually does so instead she asks my dad if I had anything to read.

"Yeah, he's got a book to read," he says. "Go on, grab your book and get some reading done."

I guess I gave an eye roll and Svenska caught it.

"Don't roll your eyes at your father, young man, or you'll find a foot up your ass," Svenska says.

She was in a bad mood. It was probably because of the rain but that's no excuse to just snap like that especially when I didn't roll my eyes at her, I rolled them at my dad and even though my dad is her grandson he doesn't need her to protect him anymore. I'm sure she could tell she hurt my feelings because I'm not good at hiding stuff like that. "You've got a hell of a poker face kid," is what my dad always says because anytime I get upset or embarrassed I blush. This can be a real problem in school when the nuns yell at you or make fun of you for not knowing the answer to a question and then tell the class that this one doesn't care to use the brain that God gave him. When that happens I turn as red as a tomato which then lets all the kids in class know that you're ashamed and that gives them ammunition to rag on you during recess and then next thing you know you're getting into a fight in the lunch room because what else are you going to do when the whole class starts laughing at you for blushing like a tomato and you end up throwing a punch because you've got to protect your honor, don't you.

Anyway, I grabbed my book and sat down on this peely-paint rocking chair Svenska had by the window, but instead of reading I just rocked back and forth watching the rain.

"Stop playing the injured puppy, will ya?" my father said when he saw me sulking.

"No. No. He's got every right," Svenska said to him. "I'm sorry I snapped at you, but every bit of me aches on a rainy day, including my mood." She then moved from the kitchen to sit on the porch.

In the past, if we had a rainy day in Rockaway, when me and Tommy were little, Svenska woulda asked us to sit with her if she went out on the porch. We'd sway back and forth on the swinging bench and watch the rain fall while she told her stories about the love of her life, her crazy husband, Eddie Fitz, who only had eyes for her. When Svenska talks about Eddie she can also get the sad look in her eyes, and I realize nobody in my family can hide their feelings. Maybe this is where my poker face comes from.

"But he died too young," she says. "Like too many young men. Gone too soon. But it wasn't the booze that got him. No. It was the goddamn dust from cutting those stones every day is what killed him. Choked the life out of him."

That's the same thing Pop McSweeney said would be the death of him, and it was, so I've already decided I'm not going to do any work that involves cutting stones or breaking rocks when I grow up.

My dad adds, "Eddie worked under the Fifty-Ninth Street Bridge and every time I go over the bridge, I think about that time he took me into work with him. If you ever needed an excuse to hit the books, it was watching Eddie Fitz cut stone."

My dad does that a lot. When we drive down the highway and guys are working on the road laying tar on a steamy summer day or we're on a bus in the city and guys are out in the freezing cold collecting garbage or we're eating in a diner and guys are cooking over a hot stove getting yelled at by the old guy that owns the joint, he says the same thing. "You see that guy there? You think he wishes he didn't cut class so often?"

Not only was Svenska in a bad mood but my dad was moody and gloomy too, but it had nothing to do with the rain and being old and achy. It's because my mom decided not to come with us that weekend. She said she had too much work around the house, and it was too damn hot in that bungalow with everybody sleeping in one room.

"That never bothered you before," my dad said to her.

She ignored that.

"Tommy doesn't want to go either. I'll stay home to keep an eye on him," she said. "You two have a grand time. Go listen to all the old stories you love so much."

She said that in a way that makes me think she doesn't like the old stories and I could tell that hurt my dad's feelings, but he would never show it.

Anyhow, Svenska doesn't invite me to sit out on the porch with her, so I stop rocking back and forth and finally pick up my book and I have to admit, it wasn't half bad. It's about this old guy, Santiago, and this kid who used to fish with him, but the old guy hasn't caught a fish in a long time and the kid's parents make him work on some other guy's boat and now the kid can only help the old man when he comes back from fishing or in the morning before he heads out. I can tell why my mom thought I would like it because even though it takes place in Cuba, it's about fishing, which I like, and they're Catholic, like us, with pictures of the Sacred Heart of Jesus on the wall, which we have in my parents' bedroom, and the old man loves the Yankees and Joe DiMaggio, like everybody else on the planet.

23

When we got to the bungalow, Grandma looked different and sounded different too and I should have known this was gonna be a lousy weekend. Instead of jumping up to give me a hug, she waved me over to give her a kiss. I hate saying this, but she smelled weird when I leaned in to kiss her. Her voice was different too. It was very low and gravely like it was hurting her to just say hello. Maybe this is why my mom didn't want to come. She musta known Grandma wasn't feeling good and that's the kind of thing that makes my mom sad. I figured I'd ask my dad about it when we went for our walk around the neighborhood.

The walk around the neighborhood is a Rockaway tradition. It always used to be all of us. Me, Tommy, and my mom and dad walking around to all the places my parents loved down here when they first started dating. But today it's just the two of us. First stop is always Boggiano's, which is on the corner of Beach Ninety-Eighth Street across the street from Playland. They have two corner windows, one for clams, one for beers. I go to the clam window and my dad goes to the beer window. This is the first place I ever ate a raw clam and if you've never eaten a raw clam or maybe never even seen one because you live on a farm or something, they are about the grossest-looking thing you could imagine. Take the biggest snot you ever picked, the biggest lunger you ever hacked up, put them together and times that by twenty and that's what a raw cherry stone looks like. And when you shoot it, which is when you suck it off the clam shell, and you feel that thing on your tongue for the first time, you just know you're gonna gag. At least that's what happened to me. But Tommy and my dad and even my mom said that I had to man up and shoot that clam and over time I would get used to it and I'd even end up loving it. They called it an acquired taste. And guess what? They were right. Now I love them.

So that was our first stop. We split a dozen little necks and I got a grape soda and my dad got a beer. If my mom and Tommy were here, we'd go into Playland and my parents would sit on a bench and drink their beers and eat their clams while me and Tommy would hit all the rides but since it's only me and my dad, we just play a couple rounds of Skee-Ball.

I wanted to ask him about my mom and why she didn't come with us this weekend because we're standing in front of the Atom Smasher roller coaster and I know that's where he took her on their first date and he made her sit in the front seat and she nearly had a friggin' coronary, so she did, and never went on a roller coaster again in her whole life but I don't know how to ask him, so I just kept my mouth shut and followed him out of Playland and into the Irish Circle Tavern.

All the old Irish bars, like the Mermaid, where my parents met and had their first dance, are gone, but the Irish Circle is still there. We sat at the bar, and I got a Coke and my dad got a Jameson Irish Whiskey and lit his cigar. There are old people in the bar that ask my dad about Svenska and his mother and father and his uncle Andrew, who owned the gas station on the corner across from Beach Channel High School. He tells me this was a classy place back in the 1950s and your mother liked it because there were never any fights in the Irish Circle.

"This place was real lace curtain, no shanty Irish allowed," he laughs.

I looked around at these guys drinking in the middle of the day and nobody looks too classy to me. I ask him if he was shanty Irish because I know he was and he's proud of it.

"You bet your ass I was, but I pulled myself up outta there. And you'll take us to the next level," he tells me. "That's why I break your balls with the reading and the writing. Unlike the rest of us, you're going to college." He's at it again—talking about college.

"I don't care what we have to do to make it happen. You are not taking the civil service test. You get into a good college and your mother and I will figure out how to pay for it."

If you don't know, the civil service test is the exam you take if you want to be a cop, fireman, or garbage man. Our neighborhood is filled with civil servants and other guys who didn't go to college. So is the Irish Circle.

After a while I got pretty bored and asked my dad if he wanted to play shuffleboard. The bar has one of those big, long, old wooden shuffleboard games with the saw dust.

"Not today kid. Maybe if your mother was here. That was her game."

I knew that was the perfect time to ask why she didn't come with us this weekend, but I wimped out again.

We walk home in silence. The sun has set and the sky is

orange. It's my favorite part of a summer day. A little breeze blows and the American flags are flapping in front of most of the bungalows and you can smell people cooking burgers and dogs on their grills. My dad reaches out and grabs my hand. He doesn't usually do this anymore and I would have never let him hold my hand walking down the middle of Marlboro Road but since we're in Rockaway and I don't really know anybody here, it's fine. If I'm being honest, it's better than fine, it feels good, but it also makes me want to cry and I don't know why. Like I said before, all sorts of stuff is confusing me this summer.

Luckily, I'm saved from my tears when who do we see—it's Mr. Ford puttering down the block on his motorized bicycle. My dad pulls his hand away from mine to wave and say hello and I'm spared from having to explain why I'm crying for no reason. Mr. Ford waves back at us but doesn't stop to talk, instead he pulls up outside another bungalow where some old biddy, not as old as Mr. Ford, is waiting by the fence and they kiss. My mom was right. He does have a girlfriend and now we know why he put the engine on his bike because he'd never make it all the way to Rockaway if he had to peddle himself. If I was him, I would just drive the old Corvette and lose the bike altogether.

When we got home, Svenska is in the kitchen and asks if we want meatballs for dinner. Of course we want meatballs because Svenska makes the best Swedish meatballs you ever had in your whole life and it's another part of our Rockaway tradition. Saturday night Swedish meatballs. She pulls out the old meat grinder, clamps it to the kitchen counter and asks me if I'm strong enough to grind our meat. I flex and show her my biceps and she smiles. She was in a better mood now.

"Good boy," she says. "I cut. You grind."

As she cuts the meat into pieces, I stick them in the grinder and crank the wooden handle. Kinda like eating clams, the first time you do this, it's pretty gross, but as you get older, you get used to it.

We had our meatballs and soon after we ate, Svenska went to bed. My dad sat on the porch, and I did the dishes. When the dishes were done, he went back to the Irish Circle, and I went to bed. In the bungalow I sleep on this little cot in the corner under a screened-in window. It was a Saturday night in Rockaway, so lots of people were up making noise. TVs and radios were playing, cars were peeling out on Beach Channel Drive, dogs were barking and cats were fighting, and since the bungalows are so close together you can hear everything Svenska's neighbors are saying and doing. It was still crazy hot out and really sticky in the bungalow and Svenska keeps the only fan she has in her little room which meant I was gonna be sweating all night. So maybe my mom wasn't lying when she used the heat as her excuse not to visit this time. Anyhow, all of this was making it hard to fall asleep, so I picked up *The Old Man and the Sea* again and zonked out after one page.

Sunday morning Svenska made her Swedish pancakes, which is another tradition. They're like crepes, if you've never had them before, only better. Svenska's were good but not as good as when my dad makes them.

"And only a moron would share that with her, and you'd be wise to keep it to yourself young man." So, I told her they were delicious and much better than my dad's.

When we leave, Svenska is sitting on her swinging bench on the porch, and I wonder what she'll do all day now that we're gone. I guess she'll do whatever it is old people do when their families don't visit them. Who knows, maybe she has a boy-friend like Mr. Ford.

As my dad and I walked to the car he told me I had two options.

"We could hurry home and go to church with your mother, or we could go up to the beach and check on the waves." I smiled.

The waves were perfect, so he grabbed his old army blanket from the trunk of the car, and we put it down on the sand and we went body surfing for almost two hours then lay on the army blanket and let the sun dry us since we didn't have any towels. I really wanted to ask him about my mom and why she didn't come with us, and this was the perfect moment to ask because it was just the two of us and everything was so quiet, and he was in a good mood because he loves swimming in the ocean and lying in the sun. Maybe that's why I didn't ask. I didn't want to ruin his mood. So instead, I went back into the ocean and swam out past the break and floated around on my back. It's a great feeling when you float up and down with the rolling waves and you forget about everything going on in your life. All you see is the blue sky above and you can barely hear anything, even the waves crashing or the little kids laughing and playing in the surf. It's almost like you're in another world or in a dream and you feel free from yourself. And this summer, that's a good place to be.

But that good feeling ends when I think about the movie *Jaws* and how I'm a perfect target for a hungry shark bobbing up and down on the sea like a sitting duck. And even though my dad tells me there's never been a shark attack in Rockaway and didn't the Big Guy swim a mile out every day and never saw a shark in all the summers he spent out here, I still swam back in closer to shore and body surfed until my dad waved me in.

He had built a sandcastle while I was in the ocean and was sitting at the water's edge just watching as the waves crept closer and closer to his castle. I sat down next to him, but he didn't say anything to me. He was just staring at the castle. So that's what I did too. We both watched as the first swashes reached the base of the castle causing the front wall to start to crumble. The tide was coming in, so each new set of waves did more and more damage until one really big wave came in and overtook the whole thing. I jumped up as the sea rushed in, but my dad just sat there and let the water wash over him. The backwash then carried what was left of the castle back out to sea.

"That's the kind of thing that would break your mother's heart, wouldn't it?" he said with a little laugh. "The temporary nature of things."

"Here today, gone tomorrow," I say. My dad just nods but doesn't get up because he's deep in thought, as they say.

I don't want to think about what he's thinking about because you can just tell it's sad and it's probably about my mom. So instead, I get to thinking about "Here Today, Gone Tomorrow," which is also the name of one of my favorite Ramones songs. It's one of their slower and sadder songs. It's on the *Rocket to Russia* album and it's the track right after "Rockaway Beach" on side one. That's probably why I know it so well because when Tommy first got that album, he played it at least a hundred times a day. Tommy loved the Rockaway Beach song because it's obviously a great song and our family loved Rockaway Beach even before the Ramones did.

Finally, my dad stands up, his castle now nothing but a little hump, and he says it's time to get back to the real world. So, we jump in the car and say goodbye to Rockaway Beach. Rock, Rock, Rockaway Beach. Rock, Rock, Rockaway Beach. We say goodbye to Rockaway Beach.

24

A week later, we say goodbye to Mr. Ford. He was in his garage working on his '57 Vette and just fell down and died.

"Well, that's how I'd like to go. Doing something I love," my dad says. "Did you ever tell your mother we saw him last weekend in Rockaway?"

"No. I totally forgot. Mom, you were right, he had a girl-friend and we saw him kissing her on the sidewalk."

"Is that true?" she asks.

My dad nods.

This seems to make my mom happy.

"Good for him," she says.

"Do you think his kids will show up to bury him or will he be one of the old timers who has an empty church for his funeral?" I ask.

"Well, I would think his girlfriend from Rockaway will be there," my dad says.

"Did he ever talk to you about his family?" my mom asks.

"No. Other than to say they all moved away and live very busy lives."

"Too busy to ever visit their father apparently," she says.

My dad shrugs and of course the thought of Mr. Ford's kids never coming to visit him in all the years we've lived across the street from him brings the gloom to my mom's eyes.

"Why don't we go then?" my dad offers. And my mom nods, then smiles and I feel good because they're going to do something together, even if it is a funeral.

But the good feeling doesn't last because my dad didn't realize he had to work that day. I think this was an honest mistake, but my mom was still pissed and that led to another big fight.

So, guess who had to go instead? On any other day, I might tell her I don't want to go to a funeral for some old guy I'm not related to, even if he did let me and my friends hang out in his garage and look at his old Vette, because I go to old man funerals all the time as an altar boy and they can be super sad when they're for lonely old guys like Mr. Ford because the church is usually empty but I didn't tell her that because she's mad at my dad and I don't want to make her mad at me.

To my surprise it wasn't an Eleanor Rigby funeral, and the church was filled with Mr. Ford's friends and family, and this made my mom happy. She had the same worries I had that Mr. Ford's busy kids wouldn't be there to bury him. But they were. One of Mr. Ford's daughters made a speech from the altar and told stories about who he was as a young man and how he fought in World War One and how he never talked about it with anyone and how they only just discovered all the medals he won because they were hidden in his closet and they only found them because they were looking for a pair of shoes to bury him in and what a good father he was and how he encouraged all his kids to go out into the world and travel and have adventures and that's what they did but in the end this made her sad because she and her brothers and sisters never made time to come back home to see him and now he was gone, but in his own way that's what he wanted for them.

I looked around the church to see if I could find Mr. Ford's girlfriend from Rockaway but she was nowhere to be found. I spent the whole Mass wondering if she even knew he was dead. What if no one knew about his girlfriend? Who would tell her Mr. Ford had died? I want to ask my mom if we can drive to Rockaway after church and go check on her but that would just be weird if some little kid showed up at your house with his mom to tell you your boyfriend had died.

Instead, on the way home from the funeral, my mom wanted to go to her favorite bakery as a treat to me for going with her to the funeral. I know you shouldn't complain about your mom taking you to a bakery to get cookies and cakes, but this bakery is in Woodside which means we have to drive all the way back to our old neighborhood in Queens and it's gonna steal another two hours away from hanging out with my friends on a perfect summer day.

My mom loves Woodside and always says she wishes we never left, even if it was her idea to move to Long Island.

"I don't know why you miss it so much. We had a tiny little apartment and no backyard," I tell her.

"True, but I had friends in Woodside." She says that like she doesn't have friends now. But she does. Lots of friends, all the moms from school and the ladies from church and even some of the old biddies on our block.

We drove up to our old apartment building and park, but we didn't go in. My mom just sits in the car and stares at the long walkway that leads to the front doors, and I could see the old memories are dancing in her head.

"Oh, the Boulevard Gardens," she says with a sigh. The Boulevard Gardens was the name of our old building, and I was born in Boulevard Hospital, but I have no idea what boulevard either place was named for. I asked my mom once and she just started singing this old song. "I walk along the street of sorrow, this boulevard of broken dreams." Then she laughed.

We used to visit a lot when I was little because she still had a bunch of friends that lived here, but like us, they've all moved away which is why I can't understand her getting sad about all her old friends in Woodside when none of them live there anymore. And it's not like we moved to California. We moved one town over the Queens borderline.

"You moved three seconds into Nassau County just to say you live on Long Island, so you did," Pop McSweeney would say.

When we got to the bakery, it too was gone. There's a "for rent" sign in the window. My mom doesn't say anything, she just nods to herself and we drive by but I know what she's thinking—everything from her past is disappearing. I also know what I was thinking—two hours wasted on a perfect summer day, and I've got no cakes or cookies to show for it.

Luckily, on the ride home, we see a Dunkin' Donuts on Rockaway Boulevard and stop to get a dozen donuts and some munchkins. Inside I'm smiling because I'd much rather have a jelly donut from Dunkin' Donuts than some rugelach from the bakery, but I don't tell my mom this.

As we drive past Kennedy airport, we also stop at the fruit guy and pick up two watermelons. He's there every summer in the same spot selling his watermelons out of the back of his truck. He's a funny guy with really big muscles and he jokes around with my mom about how pretty she is and when he tells her that, she smiles for the first time today. When we get back into the car with our watermelons, my mom says she needs to stop by the office to get something.

She works at JFK for the FAA in a new brick building that's right off the main road you take into the airport. Like I said before, I don't know what she does there, but I know she works with lawyers and anytime someone makes a joke about how everybody hates lawyers, she says some of them are very nice.

When she goes inside, I wait in the parking lot. When you're this close to the airport, you can't believe how loud the planes are overhead or how low to the ground they are. From where we're parked it seems like the planes might hit the top of my mom's office even though her building is only five stories tall.

I climb onto the roof of the Shit Mobile and lie down on my back to get a better look up at the planes. A few TWA planes and a Pan Am jet fly right over me and they're so close you can smell the jet fuel and I think to myself this must be what it was like for my dad and his friend hiding in the bushes at LaGuardia or Henry Hardware when the Green Acres Mall was an airport, and he could wave to Charles Lindbergh and Amelia Earhart. I try waving to the pilots too but these planes are too big and fly over so fast, I can't see anyone in the cockpit. All of a sudden, I hear this one plane that is so much louder than the others and I immediately know what it is because anytime it flies over our house the windows in our living room rattle, and we run out to the front lawn and look up into the sky to check it out. It's the SST. The Concorde. The fastest plane there is. I know "SS" stands for "supersonic" but I don't know what the T stands for. Maybe Turbo.

I'm in the perfect position to see it up close. As the SST flew right over me the entire car shook, and it felt like it might even knock me off the roof. I wave to the pilots and I swear to you, even though it was going overhead so fast, I could see into the cockpit and one of pilots waved back. How cool is that? I wonder if when I'm an old man I'll be telling this story every time I go into the hardware store. Probably.

My mom loves her job and when she comes back out to the car she tells me, "Thank God I have this job. I think I'd go crazy without it."

"How come?" I ask her.

"Because there's more to life than cleaning a house in the suburbs."

Of course, this reminds me of her conversation at the bar on St. Patrick's Day about the dreams a young girl has, and I can see the sadness in her eyes so on the drive home I ask her about her life before she got married and had us kids because she loves to tell me those stories and they always make her smile. She starts with the story of her first job in Manhattan working for the Metropolitan Life Insurance Company.

"They would hire all us girls from the Catholic high schools to come down there after class and work in their file room down in the basement. And on Fridays we were allowed to eat in their cafeteria. Oh, you should have seen it. We thought it was so fancy and sophisticated. All the men in their suits and the secretaries in their dresses. That was my first real exposure to how the other half lives."

She says she regrets not going to college, but it wasn't really an option back then. "Girls in the 1950s became teachers, nurses, secretaries, or nuns." It's a good thing she didn't become a nun because she would have been terrible at it because you've got to be mean and nasty, and she isn't either one of those. She tells me about the elevated train that used to be on Third Avenue, the same one she took with Pop McSweeney when he got his paycheck, and how she and her girlfriends would take it home to the Bronx after working at Met Life. She said those old elevated train stations had these big rusted pot belly stoves and in the winter all the girls would stand around them to keep warm because they were all wearing their Catholic school skirts and they'd always be freezing in those damn things. Then some stupid boy would come up and spit on the stove to watch his lunger fry, bubble and steam from the heat and the girls would scatter. Again, she'd talk about looking into the apartments you could see from the train windows but now, being a teenager, she wasn't looking for the families and the mothers and fathers and the kids. Now she was looking at all the single people having a good time.

"You'd see all sorts of different folks living their lives, having parties, dancing, and carrying on. My girlfriends and I would tell each other that after graduation if we didn't get married and move to Fifth Avenue, we'd all get an apartment like that and throw parties and sit on the fire escape on hot summer nights and have our drinks and smoke our cigarettes and soak up the sounds of the city."

But they never did. She lived at home in the Bronx until she married my dad and right after their wedding they moved to North Carolina when he got called back into the Army to serve at Fort Bragg. She says she didn't want to leave New York because at that time she was working at an advertising company on Madison Avenue, and she adored it. She says that was her favorite job because she loved being around creative people and it's also where she met her two best friends, Penny and Pat. Pat lived in the Boulevard Gardens and that's how we ended up living there too. Penny was really beautiful, and all the guys loved her and when she and my mom went out after work, they never had to pay for any of their drinks. If the guys were ugly or wore cheap suits, Penny would turn down their drinks and tell my mom, "Since when do peasants storm the castle." My mom thought that line was so funny—even though we were peasants ourselves without a pot to piss in.

Penny is my godmother and actually ended up marrying a really rich guy and moved to Chicago years ago. They have a lot of money and live in a super fancy building, but not as fancy as the buildings on Fifth Avenue that my mom used to dream of but pretty damn close. Penny never sends me anything on my birthday which is basically the most important thing a godparent is supposed to do. Tommy's godmother is my mom's other best friend, Pat, and Pat always buys Tommy something cool like a new baseball mitt or football helmet or hockey stick on his birthday. So, when it comes to godmothers, I got robbed.

When my Mom had to quit the job at the advertising company to go to North Carolina, she couldn't find a new job down there because I guess they don't like Catholics in the South.

"Whatever you do, don't put all those Catholic schools on your resume, with the St. This and the Blessed That, because if they see that shit down there, they'll ask you if you believe in the infallibility of the Pope and that's a sure sign they're not going to hire you." This is what her old boss from the advertising company told her because he had been in the army down south too, but she didn't listen to him.

"And sure enough, they asked me about the Council of Trent."

"What does that mean?" I asked her.

"It meant I wasn't getting the job." She laughed. "But the good news was, I told your father we need to start saving up if we're gonna start a family. And to do that, I need a job. So, I went back to New York and got my old position back at the ad company. And of course, my old boss told me, 'What did I tell you? Those crackers down there hate the Catholics.'"

We drove home with our doughnuts and watermelon, and she points out where a plane crashed on the side of the road a few years ago. The crash site was just across the street from the airport and the plane was almost home, but I guess it was a foggy night and the pilots couldn't see the runway lights. Luckily, it was late at night and there were no cars on Rockaway Boulevard or even more people could have been killed. My mom does the sign of the cross and tells me to do the same.

"Say a little prayer, will you."

So, I do. "Dear God, I pray that everybody who died in that crash didn't feel any pain and I hope they're all in heaven. And if there were any little babies, I hope they already got baptized."

While I'm at it, I say a little prayer for Pop, Mr. Ford, and even one for Matt Fat the Water Rat since he's been on my mind. My mom is always making us say quick little prayers like that anytime we see or hear a fire truck racing to an emergency or we drive past an accident on the highway.

"Everybody loves to watch a fire or gawk at a car crash, but you've got to remember there's usually somebody getting hurt, or worse, when we see that. So, say a little prayer for them too."

Then I say one last little prayer for my mom.

"Dear God, please let my mom be happy and please make

her see that there are good things in her life today and please don't let her keep thinking about how things used to be better because maybe they weren't as good as she remembers and even if they were better back then please help her not to think about it all the time because it keeps making her sad. Amen."

25

My dad and I were supposed to go fishing the next day but I ended up having to sit around for hours waiting for him to come home because he made an arrest that night and had to go to court this morning, so he didn't get home until almost noon. He asked if I would mind if he took a nap for a few hours and I said sure because I know if he doesn't take a nap he'll be in a shitty mood and if he's in a shitty mood on the boat, he'll yell at me the whole time.

"You're not gonna catch any goddamn fish if you don't have your goddamn sinker on the bottom," or "You're never gonna learn to be a real goddamn fisherman if I have to keep baiting your goddamn hook for you," or when I keep reeling up to check my bait, he'll tell me, "You can't catch any goddamn fish if your goddamn line isn't in the goddamn water." Luckily, he took a two-hour nap and when we drove to the marina, he was in a great goddamn mood.

We drifted along Reynolds Channel in the *Sea Ya Later* with our lines in the water, our sinkers on the bottom, our spearing and squid on our hooks, and waited for the fluke to bite. My dad smokes his cigar and drinks his can of Budweiser while I drink my can of Welch's and eat my peanut butter and jelly sandwich. We floated past the last of the old bay houses, which sit on stilts, either in the middle of the bay or on the edges of the marshes. A few of the bay houses are still being used but most of them have been abandoned and are falling apart.

"Being reclaimed by the sea," my dad says.

Once when we were little, Tommy had to take a crap while we were fishing, which normally wouldn't be a big deal. In the past, if you had to take a crap, you would jump in the water, pull your shorts down and just shit in the bay, but after Tommy saw *Jaws*, he was too afraid to float in the sea with his ass hanging out because he was sure a shark would sneak up on him and bite his balls off.

My dad told him, "I guarantee you Thomas, there are no sharks in this bay and if by some freak of nature, there is a shark in these waters, he is not going to want to go near your ass while you're dropping a deuce."

Tommy wasn't convinced, so my dad pulled up to the dock of one old bay house and told Tommy to ask the owner if he could use the outhouse. Tommy was still little then and not as tough as he is now and didn't want to go alone.

"You're not gonna come with me?" he asked our dad.

"No. Unless you need me to wipe your ass for you," my dad joked.

So, I went with him instead. Besides, I wanted to see what one of those bay houses looked like up close. My dad tied up to the small floating dock and me and Tommy climbed the old wooden ladder up to the deck that wrapped around the house. We knocked on the door, but there was no answer. Tommy told me to stay on the lookout just in case somebody came out while he went to use the outhouse. The houses have no electricity and no plumbing so if you have to take a crap, you have to use the outhouse. If I lived here and I had to pee, I would just pee off the deck into the water, because the outhouses are connected to the main houses by a long skinny dock with no railing that extends out the back into the tall marsh grass and if it was dark out and you had to pee in the middle of the night, it would be way too scary to have to walk the plank all the way back there. It was even a little scary that day and it was in the middle of a perfect summer day. My dad jokes, "I'm sure many a drunk in need of a late-night piss found themselves falling into the marsh trying to make their way to those outhouses."

When Tommy went to do his business, I really wanted to go inside the house and look around, but like I said, it was kinda scary, so I just looked through the screen windows. It was just a simple little room with old wooden furniture, but you could tell someone still lived there because there was an ashtray with cigarette butts, half a mug of coffee and an unfinished crossword puzzle sitting on the table by the window.

I was so tempted to yell to Tommy that someone was coming and watch him have to make a run for it while in mid-shit, with his shorts around his ankles, but I knew he would kick my ass for the rest of the summer, so I just stood guard and waited for him to finish.

That day, me and my dad drifted past the biggest of the bay houses, which is owned by a bunch of nuns. They have a sign on their dock, "St. Mary, Star of The Sea Retreat." Two nuns are standing on their dock with their long crabbing nets pulling blue claws out from the pilings.

My dad yells to them as we pass, "How we doin' today, Sisters?"

"Very well," they say, "How about you two, any luck?"

"Nothing so far, but who's complaining, it's a beautiful day on the water."

"It is indeed, but we'll say a prayer for you and your boy, just the same."

And I swear to God—which I know I shouldn't do, especially when telling a story about nuns—but two seconds later, I feel a tug on my line and I start reeling up a doormat fluke, the biggest I've ever seen. If you don't know, a fluke is a flat fish that swims on the bottom of the sea and has both of his eyes on one side of his face. For a fluke to be a keeper, which is a fish you can keep, it has to be at least fifteen inches long. If he's too small, a shorty, you have to throw him back but this thing on my line has got to be twenty-eight inches at least. My dad yells at me to try to keep him just below the surface of the water, so he can get the net under him because he's too big to just pull into the boat. A few years ago, my dad hooked one this big and Tommy couldn't get the net under him in time and the hook ripped from the fluke's mouth and the doormat was gone. You can imagine how pissed my dad was. Like all fishermen, he still talks about the doormat that got away. So, this afternoon, he's determined to get this big boy into the boat. Thankfully, he nets the fluke and pulls him in and there's no need for him to get pissed off and start cursing especially since we're still close enough to the nuns for them to hear him.

The fluke is huge, and just like the saying goes, he's as big as a doormat. The nuns cheer and wave as we drift away, and I wonder if the sisters at my school are like that during the summer. Do they smile and wave and say prayers for fishermen or are these two nuns special? Maybe that's why they get to come to the bay house retreat because they're the nice ones. Or maybe they're nice and friendly because they get to spend time out here on the water and everyone knows people who live by the water are happier than those that don't. If that's the case, I'll say a little prayer that the Bull gets invited to the Star of Sea Retreat next summer. Not for her sake, but for ours.

After my dad gets the hook out of the doormat's mouth, he checks to make sure we've drifted far enough away from the nuns before he grabs the fluke by the tail and smacks his head down onto the deck two times to knock him out. As much as I love fishing, I hate this next part. He takes out his filet knife and stabs the fluke behind his head and then begins to cut the fluke up, removing the two meaty sides of the fish. When he's done, he throws the head, spine, and tail back into the bay for the seagulls and crabs to have at it and throws our dinner into the cooler with his Budweiser and my grape soda.

Before heading back to the marina, we stop at a small beach just past the Cross Bay Bridge in Rockaway. I hop off the bow with a dock line and tie the boat up to the old wooden stilts of a bay house that washed away years ago. This is my dad's favorite clamming spot and he's been coming here since he was a kid. We walk into a few inches of water and squirm our feet down into the muddy bottom feeling for clams. When you feel one with your toes, you reach down with your hands and dig him out. You're not allowed to eat these clams because the water here has been polluted for years. Because of that, no one clams here anymore which means there are tons of them. The big clams are called cherry stones or chowders and the small ones are called little necks. My dad loves to tell me how the little necks got their name from Little Neck, Long Island, which used to be a famous clamming spot. Even though we have to throw our clams back, my dad still likes to come here and dig them up. And so do I. If we were fishing for striped bass, we could use them for bait but since we only fish for fluke we just toss them back home to the sea.

He says, "I can remember standing in this exact spot when I was your age, doing this exact thing. Me and my brother and our friends digging our feet into the muck and pulling out clam after clam. We'd sell them to the fishermen on the bridge for a few cents a pop. A few dozen clams and you could make yourself two or three bucks and this was right after the war and that was a lot of money to a twelve-year-old kid back then."

On the drive home from the marina, we're both quiet and tired from being on the water all day. We smell like fish and our skin is salty. The windows of the Shit Mobile are open, and the sun is setting and it's nice and quiet and I'm happy, but then it finally happens—my dad asks about my mom. He wants to know how her mood was when we went to Mr. Ford's funeral.

"How did she seem?" he asks.

"Fine, I guess. Why? Is something wrong?"

I think to myself—finally, we're going to talk about what's going on between the two of them but he doesn't answer the question. He just says, "The only reason to get married is to have kids, remember that."

That seemed like a strange bit of advice to give your son, but I could tell he was in a weird mood and when your parents are in a weird mood, that puts you in a weird mood, so I just shut my mouth, looked out the window and started singing that Cheap Trick song to myself. "Mommy's alright, daddy's alright, they just seem a little weird. Surrender, surrender, but don't give yourself away. "

When we got home, I was too tired to do anything other than lie in front of the fan and watch TV but my dad asked me if I've done any reading today and he didn't like my answer.

"When would I have done any reading? I was with you on the boat all day."

"So, after I treat you to a day of fishing and clamming, you're gonna be a wiseass?" he says. I didn't think I was being a wiseass but he did, and he got pissed so I was sent up to my room to go bury my face in a book.

Maybe it was because I spent the day fishing and clamming, but I really got into *The Old Man and the Sea* and finally finished it. And I've got to admit, I actually liked it, even if it was pretty sad. You see, the poor old guy Santiago finally catches a fish, and it's a real big one, so big he can't bring it into his boat so he ties it up to the side, but before he can bring it back to shore, the sharks attack and eat the whole thing and by the time the old man gets back to the docks there's nothing left but the bones and the whole journey of catching the fish and fighting the sharks nearly kills the old man. And that's it. That's how it ends. For some reason, the old man reminded me of Pop McSweeney. He had his job building the Lincoln Tunnel, a job he was so proud of, and that's the thing that he said would be the death of him. And it was. You got to wonder why the old guys do it.

26

Summer was almost over and my mom must have been clueless of this because she asked me to stay home and watch some of the US Open tennis match with her. She's in love with John McEnroe. He's Irish and he's from Queens and all summer she's been talking about this match he had against the Swedish guy at Wimbledon. I guess she watched it when we were in Montauk and "had the house to myself for once." She says it was the greatest match of all time except for the fact that McEnroe lost and she's hoping Johnny Mac makes it back to the finals to get his revenge against the Swede. I can tell she wants the Irish guy to beat the Swedish guy because she sometimes gives my dad the business about being part Swedish. But when you're looking at the last days of summer you're not about to sit inside and watch tennis with your mom. I mean, maybe if it was raining, but on a nice day, no shot.

When I got home from dinner, my mom was in a great mood because Johnny Mac had won. She said she didn't have anything in the house for dinner and asked if I wanted to go to Friendly's. Friendly's is a really good restaurant and not just because it's also an ice cream shop. They make my favorite hamburgers and they cut them in half like a sandwich. Anytime my mom makes hamburgers at home I make her cut them in half, but they never taste as good as Friendly's. My dad doesn't like Friendly's so he said he's gonna stay home and make himself a sandwich.

"But didn't I just say, we don't have anything in the fridge," my mom said.

"I'll manage," he said. And then there's silence.

Me and my mom sat at a booth instead of the counter. Linda Leary and Paulie Fontana, the high school sweethearts who make out on the corner under our streetlight every night both work here. Linda waits tables and Paulie scoops the ice cream. Even here, while they're working, they keep finding moments to kiss.

"Those two can't get enough of each other, can they?" she asks. I shrug.

"Ah, to be young and in love," she adds.

I shrug again, but then I realize this is an opening and ask, "Is that what you and Dad were like when you were young?" She didn't answer me for a few seconds, but then she does.

"Yes, we were."

"How come you're not like that now?"

"I don't know," she says. "Things change."

There it is again, things change. Now I'm really wishing we sat at the counter because then I could just stare ahead and watch Linda Leary grabbing plates from the kitchen window after the cook rings the bell but when you're sitting across from your mom in a booth the only thing to look at is her face and if she's talking about things changing she's gonna be sad and that's a shame because she was just in such a good mood because Johnny Mac beat the Swede but I had to ruin it by asking questions.

Luckily for me, Linda Leary brings our hamburgers along with her big smile and tells my mom she likes her hairstyle, and this put my mom in a better mood.

"I like that girl," my mom says. "She's pretty too. Do you think she's pretty?" I do but I don't answer. I just shrug.

My mom then asks if I've ever kissed a girl. I say no. Then she wants to know if I want to kiss a girl. I shrug again because of course I want to, but I don't want to talk to my mom about that. I want to talk to her about my dad and why things change and why don't they kiss anymore but I'm afraid to ask any more questions.

"What's with you tonight? All this shrugging. It's not like you. You OK?"

"Yeah, I'm fine," I say. But I'm not.

When we go to the ice cream counter, Paulie Fontana gives me an extra scoop.

"From one Marlboro Road kid to another," he says with a smile, and I can see why him and Linda are a couple. Two nice teenagers who smile a lot. Maybe it's because of all the hours making out on the corner under the streetlight or maybe it's getting to work in an ice cream shop and getting free cones and sundaes. Probably both.

It started raining during dinner and it's raining even harder when we run to our car in the parking lot. On the drive home, my mom is nervous behind the wheel. She isn't a very good driver because she didn't learn how to drive until we moved out to Long Island and driving is one of those things you can't be very good at if you learn it too late in life, like a jump shot, or so my dad says. The Shit Mobile's wipers don't work so well and it's really hard to see out the front windshield and now it's thundering and lightning and the wind has kicked up and the branches of the trees on the streets are whipping in all different directions and of course a teenager in a souped-up Chevy Nova goes speeding by us in the opposite direction spraying a huge puddle of water onto the driver's side window and it scares my mom so much that she screams out loud which then scares me and I drop that free second scoop of ice cream onto the floor. She then slows down to five miles an hour because now the windows are fogging up and she's yelling at me to find something to wipe the glass with, so I kick the scoop under the seat, take off my sneakers and pull off my socks. I give my mom one sock and I take the other and we both try to clear the foggy glass but as soon as we do the fog comes back. She then bangs her hands on the steering wheel and screams "Fuck! Fuck! Fuck!" I've barely ever heard hear her use the f-bird before, let alone three times in a row, and I have to admit it scared me more than her scream did.

When we finally turn onto Marlboro Road, tragedy strikes. It was the craziest thing you ever saw, not that we could see much it of it through the fogged-up window. A bolt of lightning shot down from the sky and struck one of our maple trees. And not just any maple but my Jesus poem maple. My mom slammed on the brakes but because of all the rain, the brakes locked, and we skidded across the street and smashed up over the curb and into the chain-link fence that surrounds the Flynn's front yard. My mom hit her head on the steering wheel and got a cut across her forehead and the blood was streaming down her face but she musta been in shock because she didn't seem to notice. Instead, she got out of the car and just stood in the middle of the street in the middle of the downpour and watched as our Jesus maple cracked in half and slowly fell down onto the pavement. As I got out of the car to see what was happening, she just stood there with the blood and the rain pouring down her face. She reached out and took my hand and held it.

"Are you OK?" I asked her.

"No," she said. "I'm as far from OK as you can be."

My parents got home from the hospital late that night. I was in bed when I saw them pull up. I was at my spot in the window staring at what was left of our maple. The town had come and cleared the fallen tree from the street. Instead of the O'Neil boys carrying it off to burn in their fireplace, the town brought the big woodchipper and all they left was the stump. When my dad parked the car, my mom got out and hustled right up into the house. My dad stayed outside for a while to study the stump. I'm not sure what he was thinking about, but he was out there for a while.

My dad slept on the couch that night. My mom slept in their bed. At some point, during the night, I snuck into bed with her, and she was still up. She said she couldn't sleep because her head hurt. She got five stitches in her forehead, and it was pretty nasty looking.

"And what the hell is that going to look like when those stitches come out," she said.

I told her she's still gonna be pretty. She told me to go to sleep. I said we'll have matching scars because I have the one above my eye from that time when Tommy threw me across the room and into the table at Grandma from the City's apartment. She told me to go to sleep again.

As we lay there, neither one of us sleeping, she said one last thing. "This scar on my forehead will be a daily reminder of your father's neglect."

27

It's quiet in our house this morning. My mom is still in bed. Tommy is nowhere to be found. My dad is home and making breakfast but he's not talking, and I can't tell what kind of mood he's in after last night. He's got a much better poker face than me, my mom, or Svenska. I'm sitting at the table eating my eggs and fried baloney and staring at a framed picture of JFK and the speech he made when he became president that hangs in our kitchen.

All Irish families have pictures of John Fitzgerald Kennedy up in their houses. Grandma from the City gave us this one because she really loved JFK and on top of that, her maiden name was Fitzgerald because her dad was Eddie Fitz, the drummer and stonecutter who broke Svenska's heart when the dust choked the life out of him.

A few years ago, I tried to look up the Fitzgeralds in the phone book thinking I could call them and see if we were related to the Kennedys in some way, but there were so many Fitzgeralds listed that I figured there's no way we could all be related. But when I asked my grandmother, she said, "Of course we are, somewhere back in Ireland, long before the famine, long before the English persecuted us, the Fitzgeralds were one family."

Anyhow, I decide to ask my dad about the JFK picture and the speech as a way to break the silence. Big mistake.

"Do you know what an inaugural speech is?" he asks me.

What the hell was I thinking? I couldn't have asked him about the Yankee game instead?

"No," I say.

"Can you pronounce inaugural?" he asks me.

I try and I can't and now I know what the next hour of my morning is going to be.

"Let's go check the unabridged," he says.

That means we're headed over to a giant unabridged dictionary that sits on the radiator cover in our dining room to look up inaugural. He does this every time me or Tommy mispronounce something or we don't know the meaning of a word. Inaugural is a double whammy—I don't know what it means and I can't pronounce it. If he tries to do it to Tommy now, Tommy just ignores him and walks out of the room.

"Being a moron isn't something to be proud of," my dad will yell after him as Tommy heads up the stairs. "Advertising your stupidity to the world is not an asset. Broadcasting your ignorance isn't a redeeming personality trait. Do you understand any of that? No, of course you don't because you don't care enough to learn!" he adds.

My guess is Tommy does understand but doesn't care.

"Antidisestablishmentarianism" is the longest word in the dictionary, by the way. I know that because one night during dinner I had the bright idea of asking my dad what was the longest word in the dictionary. After looking it up in the unabridged, it took me almost three months to finally be able to pronounce it. When I challenged Louie to see if he could pronounce it, he said I was an idiot because everybody knows "supercalifragilisticexpialidocious" is the longest word in the dictionary. Again, I asked my dad about this and he tells me to look it up and when I do, it's not in the unabridged and my dad says, "Of course it's not because it's not a real word."

Another word that got me into a lot of trouble was "aluminum." A few years ago, I asked for an aluminum bat for Little League, but I couldn't pronounce that one either. As you can tell, I'm not so good at pronouncing certain big words and it drives my father crazy because he says I just rush right over the word instead of taking my time and sounding it out.

"Pronounce the words as you speak the words." He repeats to me over and over as I try to say "aluminum" but it comes out as "aliminum" or "alnominum" or "anilunim."

"How can I buy you something if you can't even pronounce it?" he asks me.

So, I practice over and over, breaking it down. Al-um-in-um. When baseball season is almost over and we've got one lousy game left I finally pronounce it properly and I get my new aluminum bat, only to strike out every time I used it.

Anyway, we look up inaugural which means "marking the beginning of an institution, activity, or period of office" and it only takes me a few tries to learn how to pronounce it.

My dad is pleased. He gives me another nod, another smile, another piece of fried baloney and then asks, "So what did you want to know about JFK?"

At this point, I want to say "I could care less about JFK. I just want to go out and play with my friends." But I don't. So instead, I decide to take this moment to finally ask him about my mom.

"How come mom didn't come with us to Rockaway last weekend? And how come you didn't go with us to Friendly's yesterday? And how come you slept on the couch last night? Is it because you guys are getting divorced?"

"Divorced? Where the hell did you get a nutty idea like that?"

I shrug. Then he says, "When two people are married, sometimes they fight because they don't see eye to eye on everything. That's normal. But that doesn't mean you get divorced. Let's say you got a bum knee. What are you gonna do? Cut your leg off? Be a peg leg? You think you'd walk better with a half-a-leg than with a bum knee? No, of course not. So, you walk with a limp, and you live with it."

I nod. "And I don't even want to hear that word come out of your mouth again. Now do me a favor and go out and play with your friends, will you? I think you need some fresh air. Jesus Christ!" He barks at me.

I know Catholics don't usually get divorced, but I guess they don't even like to talk about it.

But that night, my mom was packing a suitcase. I watched her from the bedroom door, but she didn't see me. I knew we weren't going on a trip so I knew her suitcase could only mean one thing—she was leaving. I guess she'd rather have a peg leg than a bum knee. I was about to knock on the door and beg her to stay when the phone rang. My mom answered it.

"Hello," she said.

28

Pop McSweeny had died. The doctors said he had some kinda lung disease. Pop knew it all along, the Lincoln Tunnel would be the death of him.

29

Today we started at the funeral home then went to St. Angela's for Mass. This is the church in the South Bronx where my mom got baptized, received her first Holy Communion, had her Confirmation, married my dad, and now said goodbye to her father. Knowing her, all of those memories came back to her as she sat in the pew and sobbed.

We then drove to that huge cemetery in Queens off the LIE. They buried Pop in the same grave as his first wife which was also the same grave that his brother, Tom, is buried in because Tom was married to Pop's first wife before Pop married her. When Tom died from consumption, Pop stepped in. The first wife is my mom's mom, who died right after my mom's brother Kevin was born which was why she and her brothers Mike and Mark got sent to the orphanage and Kevin was put up for adoption. I know it's confusing and maybe that's why the grave is just marked by a flat little headstone in the ground. There are no names and no dates on their headstone—it just says McSweeney—so there's no way to know who's buried there unless your parents tell you. My dad says when Pop's brother was put in the ground back during the

Depression they had no money, which is why they have such a simple headstone.

"In fact, they were so poor, he's lucky to have a headstone at all," he adds.

Up on the hill, there's row after row of these huge, tall headstones that are for the rich dead people. If you've been crying all day and your eyes are blurry and you squint, all those big rich people's headstones look like they're part of the buildings in the Manhattan skyline in the distance. When I look at the big headstones I wish we were rich because when you walk by those graves you can't help but think about who those people were and what kind of great lives they lived but if you didn't know Pop and his brother and his first wife you'd just walk right past their little flat stone and not give any thought to who they were.

We go back to the bar after the burial. At this point, nobody seems sad anymore, even my mom. She's laughing with her brothers and Gilligan. Brady, one of the musicians from Pop's kitchen is there again, but today he's brought his fiddle. He played Pop's favorite song that he used to love to sing but they wouldn't let anybody sing it because this was Pop's song so today it was just an instrumental. Even without the words, it was a sad one and all the laughing stopped, and the crying started.

The man with the fiddle asked Tommy if he'd like to sing a song but Tommy said no. I don't know why he asked Tommy. He must have seen that Tommy wasn't talking to anyone and was sitting off by himself. Of all the people at Pop's wake and funeral, Tommy has been the saddest. If he wasn't such a jerk to me all the time, I might try to talk to him, but I know if I do, he'll call me an asshole or a dickhead and tell me to get the hell away from him and stop being such a pussy. So, I leave him alone and stand next to my mom and when the man with the fiddle starts to play another song she starts to dance and pulls me along with her. I can't really dance but I try anyhow because my mom is smiling as she swings me around and I love her face when she's happy.

Tommy didn't come home with us because he met some girl at the bar, and she was going to drive him home later.

"Who is she and what was she doing at grandfather's funeral party anyhow?" my mom wants to know.

"She lives in the neighborhood and just stopped in when she heard there was an open bar," Tommy said.

"Oh, great. She sounds wonderful," said my mom.

On the ride home I looked up out the back window at the streetlights and tree branches and telephone wires as they passed by and no matter what road we were on or how many turns we took, it looked like the moon was following us the whole way back to Marlboro Road. I was thinking maybe the moon was Pop giving me a signal that he was in heaven with his brother and his first wife, and he was watching us and that everything was OK and not to worry about the simple head-stone because we know who's buried there and why would we care what somebody else thinks. Your family knows and that's all that matters, so it does.

30

My mom tried to convince Tommy to take a drive with her to the Bronx today to check on Gilligan. She was hoping he might want to spend some time with his mother because "didn't my father just die and Tommy seemed sadder than all of us at the wake and funeral and wouldn't it have been nice for him and me to spend some time together after such a long heartbreaking summer," but Tommy said he had plans with that girl he met at the bar after the services. So, guess who had to go instead.

On the drive to the Bronx, she wasn't in the mood to talk so we just listened to the radio. She had on 66 WNBC, and I don't know what was going on with the DJ today, but he was only playing the saddest songs. One tearjerker right after another and they all made you want to cry, especially on a day when you're going to the Bronx to see your step-grandmother a few days after they buried Pop. As we crossed over the Throgs Neck Bridge, the DJ played that Jim Croce song about saving time in a bottle and how he wants to save every day just to spend them with this girl and of course that makes me think of how I'd love to have one more day sitting on the fire escape watching Pop smoke his pipe and listening to the crowd at Yankee Stadium. Then they play that song about the guy who's not in love anymore and there's some old picture that used to hang on a wall and it's not there anymore and how big boys don't cry, so of course that makes me feel bad about crying. Then they play the cats in the cradle song, and you don't need to think about something from your life to cry to that one because that's already the saddest song there is. Except of course, the saddest of the sad songs, the one by Terry Jacks about the seasons in the sun and every different section of the song gets sadder and sadder but the part where his papa dies really gets me going, especially when he sings the line about too much wine and too much song and now I'm thinking about how I'll never see Pop singing and dancing in his kitchen with all his friends again. And then I realize I'm doing the same thing my mom does all the time—thinking about the past and how it was better than today and that gets me worried that I'm gonna be just like her—always being sad that things change. It's all too much so I've got to look out the window, so my mom doesn't see that I'm losing it.

"You OK?" she asks.

I nod, but I don't look at her.

As we get close to the apartment there are a bunch of buildings that have been burned and abandoned and they're all boarded up, but someone has painted curtains and little flowerpots on the wood that covers where the windows used to be and that makes me sad too and I don't know why.

At the apartment, I help my mom pack up some things that Gilligan wants her to have. Pop kept a handful of keepsakes from Ireland including his wedding picture from his first marriage to my mom's mom. My mom shows me the picture and whispers that Pop is back in her arms right now.

"And that's where he belongs," she says in a whisper, so Gilligan won't hear.

Gilligan makes lunch, tuna fish sandwiches on white toast. I say I'm not hungry because what kinda kid eats tuna fish sandwiches. As they eat, I go into Pop's old bedroom and see his pipe sitting on his bedside table. I pick up the pipe and smell it and it takes me back to this room last year with me and Tommy climbing through the window to sit on the fire escape with him. I know it's a sin to steal but I take Pop's pipe and stick it in my pocket. I figure if there is a Jesus in heaven then Pop is sitting right next him and will tell him it's OK. He'd want me to have it.

I join Gilligan and my mom at the kitchen table as they're looking at old black-and-white pictures of my mom and her brothers when they were kids living in this apartment. Even though they were really poor and sometimes didn't have Pop around to take care of them, they're surprisingly well dressed in these pictures. My uncles Mark and Mike wear little sports jackets and ties and my mom is always in a dress.

"Don't be fooled. It was just for Easter, and everybody made an effort on Easter," she says. "Even if you had no money."

"You recognize that suit your father is wearing, don't you?" Gilligan asks my mom.

"So it is," My mom says, and they both laugh. It's the suit he was buried in.

Their Easter pictures were always taken in the same spot in front of the fountain with the naked ladies in the middle of Joyce Kilmer Park.

"He would make sure our hair was brushed and our clothes were clean and drag us down to stand with the tulips in front of the Sirens," my mom says.

"Oh, that reminds me. I should show you the Kilmer poem. Do you think you'd like that?" Gilligan asks me.

I want to tell Gilligan that twelve-year-old boys don't like poems, even twelve-year-old boys who have won poetry contests, but I don't because her husband is dead and she was just telling my mom she's leaving the Bronx to go back to Ireland because there's nothing here in the States for her without your father so I'll probably never see Gilligan again and if she wants to show me a poem I have to let her. So, she goes down the hallway and pulls a framed poem off the wall and brings it to me.

"Go on and read it to us, would you? It was one of your grandfather's favorites, even though Joyce Kilmer wasn't Irish."

"Read it?" I say. "Like out loud?"

My mother nods and smiles. "It's like your poem. It's about trees." Oh great.

So now I have to read this thing out loud but luckily it's very short and I can pronounce all the words. I can't really remember any of it except the last two lines.

"Poems are made by fools like me, but only God can make a tree."

Gilligan says I can keep the poem to hang in my room and I decide I will hang it, not because I like poetry but because I miss Pop and I don't have anything else of his—other than his pipe but she doesn't know that. She then gives an old black-and-white picture to my mom. This one's not in a frame but it's folded over and creased.

"Your father would have wanted you to have this." Gilligan says.

It's a picture of Pop and my mom's mom back in Ireland. Pop is so young and happy in the picture, and he looks big and strong. My mom's mom is laughing and looks pretty and, in this picture, you can actually see all her freckles. It reminds me of the wedding pictures of my own parents when they were young and happy and laughing. Maybe everybody is happy when they're young and you just get sad and fight as you get older.

"I've never seen this picture before," my mom says.

"Neither had I," Gilligan says. "I found it in the Bible he kept in his bedside drawer."

"You know who he's a spitting image of in that picture, with that big grin on his face, don't you?" my mom asks.

I know who she means. Pop looks just like my brother Tommy when Tommy used to smile. It makes sense to me why Tommy was her favorite when we were little. It's because Tommy reminded her of Pop and she loved Pop more than anything. And now she's lost the two of them.

"I'll be sure to show it to him when we get home," she says. But when we get home Tommy is still out with the girl who goes to funeral parties to get free beer.

31

Today is my birthday. I'm thirteen. Now a teenager. I guess I'm due to turn into an asshole any minute now.

Every year we have a birthday tradition where I climb up the street sign pole outside our house and pull myself up onto the sign so my dad can take a picture. The two street signs sit at the top of the pole with the Page Road sign above the Marlboro Road sign.

If you sit on the Marlboro sign and push your knees up under the Page sign, you can brace yourself and you won't fall off. When I was little, it used to drive my mother crazy because she was afraid I'd slip off and crack my skull and wouldn't that be something to not make it to your next birthday because your father insists on making you do stupid things like that. Today I cross my arms and pose, looking down at my dad in the middle of the street with his camera as he takes the shot. We've got a series of these pictures from every birthday hanging in our side door hallway. Tommy stopped posing for them years ago.

I always have a Carvel ice cream cake for my birthday and as my mom is lighting the candles, she tells me and my dad about the time I said I didn't ever want to turn into a teenager.

"Do you remember that?"

"No," I say.

"I guess it was a few years ago, Tommy had to be about fourteen and started acting out and of course your father and him got into it, yelling and screaming, and he was going on about running away and how he hated us and then I got upset and started crying and then you got upset and ran to your room and when I went in to comfort you, you said you didn't want to ever be a teenager but promised me that when you did you would never be mean to us and say such hurtful things."

Then she lit the last candle and slid the cake in front of me.

"And Kneeney, I'm going to hold you to that," she said.

I can't believe she's brought this up again. It's like they both know I'm going to change, and they don't want it to happen, and I don't want it to happen, but we all know it's gonna happen. And that sucks. But today it doesn't matter because the three of us are standing around my birthday cake and all of us are smiling and my parents seem happy again.

"Now make a wish and blow out your candles," my mom says. I make a few.

I wish that time could stand still. I wish that I could save this moment in a bottle like Jim Croce. I wish that my mom doesn't change her mind and pack another suitcase. Then I blow out my candles.

After the cake I open my present. It's more books. I guess they forgot I wanted a record player.

"We picked them out together," my mom says.

Yippee! Just what every kid wants for their thirteenth birthday. And just listen to these titles, one sounds more boring than the next—*The Sun Also Rises, A Farewell to Arms,* and *For*

Whom the Bells Tolls. So far, being a teenager is off to a shitty start.

"We figured since you liked *The Old Man and the Sea* you'll probably go for these as well," my dad says. I doubt it but I obviously don't say that. I pretend it's awesome and give my mom and dad a hug.

I lie on my bed after dinner and just hang out by myself for a while staring at the ceiling instead of looking out the window and staring at our maple tree because now our maple is gone. I'm not listening to any music because I didn't get a record player and I'm definitely not reading any of my new books for all the reasons I already gave you. I was in that kind of mood where you just want to be alone and quiet and turn your mind off.

When I finally got up, I felt different. It started when I grabbed one of my pillows off the bed. It's a little Spiderman pillow that I got for my ninth birthday, which now seems like a long time ago. A kid I'm not friends with anymore actually made it for me. His mom was big into arts and crafts, and she made these quilts with the Mother's Club at the school that they would donate to the less fortunate every year at Christmas. When I unwrapped this pillow at my birthday party the kid apologized for giving me such a lame gift but his mother forced him to do it and she made him do the whole thing, like stuffing it with the cotton balls and stitching it up but it was his idea to draw the picture of Spiderman slinging his web and write "Happy Birthday From Spidey" on it and we both agreed that Spiderman was pretty cool.

When I got this thing, I thought it was lame because who wants some homemade pillow as a birthday gift but at some point, and I don't remember when, I fell in love with it. I fell so in love that I still sleep with it every night. My mom calls it my cozy. Like Linus in Charlie Brown has that blanket, I have my Spidey pillow. But tonight, when I was sitting on my bed and looking at Spidey and his web and his happy birthday wish, I got to thinking that it's a little goofy for a thirteen-year-old kid, a teenager, to still sleep with his cozy pillow. I was thinking that it was time to grow up. Time to pack up my little kid toys, my little kid pillow, and even my little kid self. Time to pack them all up and stick them in the attic. So, I grabbed a box from the basement and said goodbye to my Spidey pillow. Then I cleared out the rest of my other childhood stuff from the bookshelves, including my Catholic Daughters of America Poetry Contest trophy, and threw it all in the box with Spidey.

As I carried the box up to the attic my mom stopped me on the stairs.

"What do you have in the box?" she asked.

"Just some stuff from my bookshelves. I needed to make some space for the new books you got me."

"Let me see what you're getting rid of," she said as she looked into the box. When she sees what I've packed, she just nods and heads off to her bedroom.

Up in the attic, I put my things in the closet next to the box of stuff my mom put up there years ago. Now Spidey sleeps with Balboa and the rest of my childhood.

32

Tomorrow is the first day of school which means today is the last day of summer. The saddest day of the year. Well, maybe that's not true this year because there were a lot of sad days this summer, but it's still a sad day. At breakfast this morning my dad could tell I was down in the dumps.

"What's with the sour puss?" he asked.

I shrugged.

"You know what you're feeling? It's called melancholia and it's another curse of the Irish," he said. "Just ask your mother." And my mom actually laughed.

But I didn't laugh because I didn't know what melancholia meant so he sent me to the unabridged to look it up. It means deep sadness or gloom. But that wasn't what I was feeling because after Pop died, I know what deep sadness feels like and this feeling I've got is different.

"It's the last day of summer and I'm sure that stinks but you're excited about school tomorrow, aren't you?" my mom asks. "Seeing all your other friends you haven't seen since June?" I nod.

"It's bittersweet." She then adds, "One thing is ending and another is beginning."

She's right. That's more the feeling I have. But I didn't know what bittersweet meant either, so I had to look that up too and it's a better description of how I feel—something pleasant but marked by elements of suffering and regret.

When I think about it, that pretty much describes this whole summer. There were plenty of pleasant moments but there was also plenty of suffering. Pop McSweeney's death being the worst day of all but also Mr. Ford dying and of course everything going on with my parents this summer has been really hard to watch but we've also had some great times together and my dad did say I was crazy to ask him if they were getting divorced and they were both sitting with me in the kitchen this morning having their coffee as I ate my bowl of no brand cereal and they seemed to be happy. So that's good. Maybe it's because my mom got her stitches out and you can barely see the scar on her forehead, so she won't have the daily reminder of my father's neglect.

So that covers the suffering part of the summer but I'm not sure what I feel regretful about. I looked up regret in the dictionary—without being told by my dad—just to make sure I knew what it meant and it means to mourn the loss or death of something. To miss something very much. And now I know what I'm feeling and what I'm missing and what I'm mourning. And it's all the same. I'm not a little kid anymore, and I'm sad that it went by too quickly. And like my mom, it breaks my heart that things have to change.

FAMILY PHOTOS

I grew up hearing my parents talk about their childhood and the stories they passed down from my grandparents and great-grandparents. The characters in *A Kid from Marlboro Road* draw from the people I knew growing up. In the following pages of Burns and McKenna family photographs you'll meet some of them.

Coming from Ireland. My grandfather Mike (on the left, holding my Uncle Jim) is the inspiration for Pop McSweeney. Like Pop's wife in the book, my grandmother Mary Catherine, seated in the middle front row, died in the Bronx when my mother was three years old.

Rockaway

Rockaway Beach 1941. My father, Ed, the skinny kid on the far right, spent every summer of his childhood on and around Rockaway Beach at Beach 101st Street.

His mother, Josephine, the inspiration for Grandma from the City, is seated next to him, and his sister Joan next to her. My dad's brother, Patrick, stands behind them.

(*above*) **My mother Mary and her brother John** pose in their Sunday best on their roof off the Grand Concourse in the Bronx, just a few blocks from Yankee Stadium.

(*below right*) **My dad in the summer of 1941.** We were always told that if you could live near the beach you'd have a better shot at happiness.

(*below*) **My mother, Mary, and her father, Michael "Pop" McKenna and Pop's dog, Prince.** Prince used to wait outside the bar on the corner of 162nd Street and Morris Avenue while Pop got his load on.

Rockaway
July. 1941

Before heading to Easter Mass, my mother and her brothers Jim and John pose in front of the Fame statue, recently restored, at Joyce Kilmer Park in the Bronx.

(*right*) **My parents met in Rockaway** in an area that used to be called Irish Town in the summer of 1961. Here is my mother, second from the left, and her friends on a crowded beach day that same summer.

(*left*) **My mom** at St. Vincent Ferrer High School on Sixty-Fifth and Lexington.

(*above left*) **My great-grandfather, Andrew, "the Big Guy,"** holding my father outside his trucking company's garage in Hell's Kitchen.

(*above right*) Wearing his white hat at Rockway Beach, the Big Guy poses before going for one of his epic swims.

(*below left*) Outside my grandfather's apartment at 441 Tenth Avenue.

(*below right*) Before the booze got the best of him, my grandfather with my father in front of the boardwalk sometime in the late 1930s.

My grandmother, **Josie**, as a teenager, posing with a friend.

Still a teenager. Josie pushing the stroller on the right in Hell's Kitchen with her newborn, Joan, and my Uncle Pat walking between her and a girlfriend pushing her own stroller.

(*right*) **My grandfather and some of the neighbors** living the bungalow life at Beach 101st Street.

(*below*) **My dad Edward on the left.** On the right, my father's sister Joan and the inspiration for Svenska, my great-grandmother, Anna Octavia Johanson.

Summer 1942

Edward   Grandma Joan